Black Jacob

BLACK JACOB

A *Novel by*

WILLIAM MAHONEY

THE MACMILLAN COMPANY
COLLIER-MACMILLAN LTD. · London

Library of Congress Catalog Card Number: 69-10640

FIRST PRINTING

THE MACMILLAN COMPANY
COLLIER-MACMILLAN CANADA LTD., TORONTO, ONTARIO
Printed in the United States of America

I wish to thank Professor Sterling Brown for his spiritual leadership, and Len Holt and Jim Lee, who realized an artist not only needs inspiration but some fatback and greens on his table.

This Work Is Dedicated to Fannie

Contents

I

I

Thursday, First Dark

THE SUN BURNING was the only thing that changed. Inert masses of vegetation grew in the ages-old swamp beside the road. Vines ran unnaturally over the ground and burdened yielding trees to form a canopy of green.

Jesse slapped hard at the gear stick and pumped the clutch, coaxing the truck to 60 and 70 mph with the speedometer needle occasionally bouncing to 80 mph. Jesse's dark glasses shielded his eyes from the red sun that hung in the sky before him. He puffed on an unlit cigarette while wrestling the driving wheel and helping the truck feel its way along the asphalt road.

Curt, the other person in the cab of the truck, looked out the window at the pine forest speeding past. For the two inside the noisy truck the world outside had become a sea of silence. At the speeds they were traveling the steering wheel of the truck responded as loosely as the tiller of a boat.

"You think the clutch will hold?" Curt asked.

"It might," Jesse said. "If we don't have to change speeds or pull any big hills we'll make it."

"What's wrong with it?"

"Too many hot-rodders use this truck. They down-gear instead of using the brake," Jesse said.

"One motherfucker that should never be allowed to use a truck or car is Cliff," Curt said.

"These machines," Jesse said, slapping the steering wheel, "are lifesavers."

"That's why we can't allow those motherfuckers to mess them up."

"You don't know your people very well."

Curt was silent and his face deadly serious.

"Sure Cliff will put a machine through hell. But when he's through he knows what that car or truck will do. He'll push it to the limit. But he'll take care of it too."

"I don't give a damn," Curt said. "There's only a few people I'll ride with. I'll take a bus before I'll ride with Cliff."

The yellow land covered with gnarled pines gradually gave way to black-earthed bogs of willow, bald cypress, tupelo and gum trees all straining under a heavy cover of gray moss.

Jesse and Curt seemed fascinated by the sun's lazy dimming and lowering.

Sensing Curt's thoughts Jesse said, "We'll get there."

"I told you we shouldn't have wasted time arguing over prices on tents and stoves."

"How are they doing?" Jesse shook his head toward the rear of the truck.

Curt switched around uncomfortably on the seat and looked

out the back window of the truck. A few loose pieces of canvas and rope shook like flags in the furious wind. "Okay, but if the wind ever gets under the canvas—goodbye tents."

"It won't be much fun setting them up in the dark. But if we have to we can. The center poles are cut and the platforms are built."

The two men looked at the red sun and seemed to search for words to break the silence.

"You won't be afraid of a little Klan riding tonight?" Jesse laughed. Once stated the fact didn't seem as horrible.

"Let them motherfuckers come. I got just what they need," Curt said.

"We might need the radio. Is it working all right?"

"Couple of days ago I called around on it."

As the afternoon breeze moved from the fields toward the low swamps the smell of the countryside's flowers filled the air. Stirring in the wind, dandelions, black-eyed Susans, wisteria and buckeye received the last rays of the dying sun.

Speeding down the highway the truck passed a panorama of plantations: cotton-white fields stretching out as far as the eye could see with groups of heavily dressed men, women and children humped over and crawling through rows of the white plants. Scattered along the fringe of the fields, in the silent world about the truck, square one-story houses of weathered board, sitting on cinder-block legs, poked up from dirt yards. Brown children waved to the truck. Cotton plants snuggled close to the shacks.

"You think the tents will be warm enough?" Curt asked.

"This is Mississippi, man," Jesse said smiling.

"Shit. It gets cold as a witch's tit down here in the winter."

"I think those wood and coal stoves we bought will do the job."

"How will the smoke get out?" Curtis' questions were posed with confidence that a reasonable answer would be forthcoming.

"Stovepipes."

"Fuel?"

"Plenty wood laying around. There's goin' to be some trouble, though. They're cutting trees off the hill."

"Erosion, huh."

"Yeah."

The road broadened to three lanes. Gas stations, sparkling shopping centers advertising everything one could imaginably want to consume, general stores, post offices and fire departments all formed nameless towns. A half-mile-long series of signs repeated the message, "Jesus Saves." Billboards advertised soaps, farm machinery and foods of all tastes.

Looking straight ahead through the hazy air into the sun, Curt proclaimed, "Jacob won't be there."

"What do you mean?"

"That nigger's got too much to lose fooling with us out at Tent City. It's one thing for him to come to rallies and make speeches. It's another thing for a BIG doctor like him to risk his GOOD name handing out pills in Tent City."

"He'll be there," Jesse said.

"Shit."

"He knows that if those people are going to vote for him Monday they've got to be alive and well. A quarantine is all we'd need."

As they rolled over the top of a hill, in the dusk they could see a matrix of lights. They rushed downhill past Greek Revival and French Provincial mansions with signs in front of them saying: Matchez School for Young Ladies, Hofstra Finishing School and Olde South Museum. The buildings faded into landscapes of shrubbery and weary trees, far back from the road. Matchez townfolk sat on porches, smoking and chatting. Workingmen walked comfortably down the road smoking their after-dinner pipes with smoke rising from them like little chimneys. Young "sports" hung around drugstores, hot-dog stands and garages (cars, along with horseshoe games and TV, were fascinations for all Matchez youth).

Curt searched bevies of unsmiling faces along the road and waved at familiar ones.

Leaving the lighted area of saloons and stores, the truck turned onto a warm-dark road. The jagged gravel crunching under the tires gave way to deep-rutted dirt. They bumped past the Elks Hall, a deserted-looking building with its belfry tall in the sky. They jolted and bounced along toward the grain elevator and signal tower, looming dark machines on the horizon. A wedge-shaped wooden sign read: "Camp Grove."

Trees and vines reached at them from the edge of the road.

"What's a damn mule doing loose on the road?" Jesse slowed down so as not to frighten the animal standing in the other lane.

"I thought I was ignorant," Curt said. "You got me beat hands down. That was a damn donkey."

Light flickered in the road. Curt reached in the glove compartment and grabbed a pistol. They saw black faces and relaxed. Curt put the black six-shot pistol back in the glove compartment. As they stopped the truck blinding flashlights were beamed into their faces flooding them with searing light. Then the lights were lowered.

Jesse opened the door of the truck and jumped out. Curt got out on the passenger's side.

The night breeze held a heavy honeysuckle smell.

"Who . . . "

"Jesse . . . "

"Jesse and Curt . . . "

Voices crisp and electric were in the air.

"Well, Jesse, you shore didn't get back none too soon. We got a nudder one for ya." A woman of substantial black flesh who wore an army jacket approached them.

"It ain't right. Lawd knows it ain't right," argued one nervous little woman. Her outstretched palm moved in sweeping motions toward furniture piled alongside the road. Arranged almost as though someone had set up house on the edge of the county road sat a coal stove blackened with a thick crust of burnt drippings, a double-bed mattress, a box bedspring, a bureau with a mirror lying detached beside it, an old grand-father clock and a upright piano that had an empty space in it where a piano roll might once have fit.

"Why the Gittens?" Jesse asked the large lady.

"Like the rest, honey. We can't rightly say. They was livin' in a condemned building. County agents tacked up a sign sayin' it wasn't fit to live in. Nicholson let dem live dere, though, and collected rent. Dey wuz a little ahind in de rent as usual. Only reason we kin see was dey done regish to vote."

An old lady and a couple of children worked at the handle of the front door.

"Get dem door knobs. De locks too. Everythin' what's ours," said a thin old fellow with a notably large forehead who stood near Jesse.

Jesse and Curt walked over and for no godly reason inspected the furniture in an action bred of futility. Old Man Gittens, who occasionally spat "bacca" juice through his rotten teeth, went to the pile of furniture and sat down on a wicker chair.

The heavy lady walked over to Jesse and Curt. "How many tents 'd you bring?"

"Ten. Along with some stoves," Jesse said.

"We jist got platforms built for three. Some menfolk prom-ised to hep, but didn't show up today."

"Well," the old lady said, coming near, straightening some boxes on top of a dresser, "dey can't put us no further than out."

Jesse and the heavy lady laughed.

Curt looked blankly at the group. "They can put you under," he said.

"We're going to be late," Curt whispered to Jesse.

Jesse looked at Curt as though in disbelief and walked toward a quiet place on the road behind the truck. Curt followed him.

Facing a darkening field Jesse softly affirmed, "Look, I appre-ciate it whenever you folks from the central committee come into town. But here, I'm running things. Anything to do with the movement, I okay. Got it?"

"All right bro'," Curt said without the least conviction.

They walked back toward the furniture.

"Let's get this furniture loaded up and move it out to Tent City," Jesse told the old couple.

"The truck's already too overloaded," Curt said.

Narrowing his eyes with disapproval, but shaking his head, Jesse indicated that he thought Curt might be right. "Okay. We'll make a couple o' trips. The people first. Then the furniture."

"We'll have to leave someone here to watch the stuff."

"The chilluns can do dat," the heavy lady said.

They loaded the old couple into the back of the truck on a pile of tents. Curt sat in the back of the open truck to allow Mrs. Moore to sit up front.

Bouncing along the road, furniture and people piled in a truck, they looked like one of hundreds of caravans moving in the Mississippi evening.

2

Doctor Jacob Blue

Jacob helped his mother downstairs. Her skin was dry like the cracked skin on a land turtle's neck.

He placed her in her usual position at the table.

"Don't you have to get downtown early today?" Leah asked.

Jacob sat at the head of the table and looked over the top of his paper at Leah. "Eight at city hall."

"Jeanne," Leah called.

Jacob flinched. So loud. Why so loud, he wondered.

A black-stockinged, black-dressed woman stuck her head in from the kitchen door.

"No breakfast for Mr. Blue."

"Some coffee," he said. "Black."

Jacob looked up from his paper at his mother whose jaws moved in churning circular motions over her food as she ate breakfast, making noises with her ill-fitting dental plates. Having registered disapproval by looking up from the paper, he returned to the gray page of type and pictures.

The war. Bombing. Cotton prices falling. The Redskins beat the Bluesocks. Teacher raped in hallway of boarding house.

Jeanne brought the coffee. Across the table Leah read the society page. He examined her dark eyes unclouded by mascara or silver-blue dyes, her wrinkled brow, sallow complexion and full lips. Contrary to other mornings, she was saying nothing to him. He wondered if her reticence this morning was a form of criticism.

Jacob gulped down the scorching black coffee.

His mother, as usual, ate her grits with sugar rather than with gravy or butter. She wore one of her flowery rayon dresses. She was a woman who still read the bible. Perhaps it had something to do with her inability to sleep. She often sat in bed all day talking to old friends, releasing a terrible flood of memories.

"I told Sheslona you could see her today," Leah said. "You can find some time to slip her in your schedule, can't you?"

"I wish you wouldn't do that. My schedule is very tight today."

"Jacob."

"Tell her to come and I'll fit her in."

Jacob looked at his wife and thought, she's getting fat. All of Leah's relatives were obese. Their stomachs—in rebellion against the loads of food or the things done to the food they had eaten all their lives—had started digesting themselves and so they suffered from ulcers.

Jacob dug into his vest pocket. He wore a sporty but comfortably functional tweed jacket and pants. He pulled out his datebook.

8:00 Meeting of Advisory Board to the City Planning
      Office
9:00 Agriculture-Stabilization Board to talk about Negro
      farmers' crop allotments
10:30 Office
6.00 Jesse—tents
7:00 Dinner

Jacob felt a tremendous weight constricting him as the week
neared its end. Friday he would keep his schedule loose and
spend more time campaigning. Thursday was the last day he'd
practice seriously that week. And after Monday, if he were
chosen as the first black Congressman from Mississippi, he
might never again practice medicine. Perhaps he could get some
young doctor into his office to keep the business going.

His morning was wasted in meetings of people who conducted studies, expressed good intentions and did nothing.
The planning board would continue to zone Negro and white
districts, slums, residential and commercial districts. The board
would continue to hide its most vital information from the
citizens. The Agricultural-Stabilization Committee would continue to allot less money and acreage to Negro farmers than to
whites until the day that there were no Negro farmers. When
everyone had given up and gone to the city, then they would
make broad moves to help the Negro farmer.

Jacob walked into the crowded waiting room.

Country people dressed in their Sunday best on Thursday sat
with their backs stiff against the bench, seemingly frozen by the
anesthetizing breath of the air-conditioned office.

"Mornin'," he said with affection.

"Mornin', Doc," the others said.

Nurse Waters was sitting behind the desk beaming beautiful
black smiles in an immaculate white uniform.

In the silent room he could hear the air conditioner. He

wondered if the silence was because of the usual fear of country people in a city doctor's office, or was this a special fear inspired by his political involvement?

"Nurse Waters," he said, taking a seat by her at the reception desk with his back to the room. "We'll need more gauze, tape, liquid soap, disinfectant, linen, Novocain, gloves, flats, suture trays, mecresin, cremomycin, saline, towels, hemostats, scissors." By her raised, questioning eyes, he knew that she understood. The weekend would probably be a rough one.

Nurse Waters left the desk and walked through the room sticking thermometers into everyone's mouths.

Jacob rose and went into a treatment room. He pulled on his white jacket.

A lady entered and he took the card from her. On it Nurse Waters had neatly printed in green ink vital statistics. "Mrs. Jackson. Temperature 100."

"What seems to be the trouble, Mrs. Jackson," Jacob said, noting the strained facial muscles and the way she sat on the edge of the chair.

"Jest sick and tired. Head aching all de time."

"Your husband living? Any children?"

"Had five young 'uns. Had two to die on me. Reckon I been married about ten years."

"Do you have a family doctor?"

"Yes suh. I usually go to Doc Tyson. Born all my young 'uns . . . but . . . "

"Mrs. Jackson, you just be comfortable, now. We're going to take care of whatever ails you." The woman's sagging flesh, her veins near the surface of her arm, dry skin, broad hips and dumpy bottom, rotten teeth, crooked fingers and broken fingernails, support stockings on varicosed legs spoke of her poverty. Her hands moved nervously to her lips and then back to her lap.

"Ain't been to Old Man Tyson in years."

Jacob picked up the phone and buzzed the nurse. "Don't forget the hemostats and mecresin," he said. He put some gum in his mouth. "Trying to break the nicotine habit," he said. "Do you smoke?" he asked.

"Smokes a little pipe with molasses 'bacca. Don't chew but I dips a little now and agin." Her stained teeth told of her habit.

"Let's take a look at you." While she undressed he checked his stethoscope and then washed his hands. "Don't suppose dippin' is the worse thing you could do. Do you have aches and pains?"

"No, but I got dese here sores on my legs."

On the scaley skin of her calf were red running sores.

"Ain't nothin' serious is it?"

"No. But it's somethin' children usually get."

"What is it?"

"Impetigo. We'll have it cleared up in no time. I'll be back in a minute."

Jacob went through one of the white doors of his office into another treatment room. He picked up the phone. "Show the next patient in here. And prepare the patient in One to have a surface ulcer on her legs cleaned up."

The doorway was filled with the body of a strapping black man. He looked like a turpentine worker.

"How do you do," Jacob said.

"Doc, when you goin' operate?"

"What?"

"When you goin' operate on me?"

"I've never met you before." Jacob wondered if the man were drunk or crazy. His pupils were red. Jacob wondered if this huge madman could've been sent by his enemies. The only weapons available were the gleaming surgical knives in the sterilizer.

"I'm ready, Doc. The pain's pretty bad." As the man came near Jacob could smell alcohol. It seemed to be dripping from his pores. Jacob hit the examining table. "Sit here."

"You goin' operate?" the fellow said, sitting on the table.

"What's your name?" Jacob had gained some calm because the man was following his instructions.

"Jim Greer."

"Roll up your sleeve."

The man obeyed. People with pained bodies could only temporarily direct their interest away from their suffering. Jacob had seen many people in pain and believed that only narcotics and religion truly salved them.

"Make a fist," Jacob ordered, taking his blood pressure. "Who referred you to me?"

"At de Charity Hospital dey told me to see you."

"What hurts?"

"Rat here," he said, pointing to his shoulder.

Jacob put his stethoscope to the man's chest, wondering if his heart were as enlarged by hypertrophy as his arm and shoulder muscles.

"You do heavy lifting?"

"Not ordinarily. Just throws cotton bales into trucks. But sometimes we gits crates o' tin. They're kind o' heavy. Weigh a thousand pounds."

"Anyone ever tell you that's too much work for a man?"

"Nobody never said I couldn't, so I did. Besides I have a partner."

Moving as one on a dark mountain trail, Jacob examined Greer's body. "Turn this way. Now that." Jacob walked briskly from the room. "Be back in a minute."

He checked with Nurse Waters to see if the other patient was ready, then reentered the room with Mrs. Jackson. He washed his hands. "We'll take care of that in no time." Jacob pulled on the skin-thin rubber gloves and scraped the scabs from the lady's legs. Then he cleaned out the sores well and dressed them. Washing his hands again Jacob said, "Where do you live?"

"Nicholson's."

"You sleep alone?"

"Sleeps wid my two youngest chullen, 'cept when my husband's home from working on de railway."

"You should sleep alone for a while. Take this until the sores clean up," Jacob said, handing her a jar of salve.

"What do ah owe ya?"

"Bring me some of that apple butter you fix out there." If she lived on the Nicholson plantation there was no question but that she couldn't pay the bill with cash. An image flashed in Jacob's mind of times he'd gone to the plantation with his mother when they'd had giant black kettles of apples boiling on fires in the yards. When he was young he'd preferred the store-bought apple butter because it was smoother, but of late he'd acquired a taste for the old-fashioned lumpy variety.

As she left, Jacob picked up the phone. "Show the next patient in. Be sure to get a card filled out on Mr. Greer in treatment room Two." When Jacob had first employed Ethel Waters he was shocked to learn one day that she was confronting patients with their old overdue bills at the reception desk. Probably a nasty habit she'd picked up in some other doctor's office. He ended it. Since then she'd been a perfect helper, sometimes taking on more than one should ever expect of a nurse.

He heard the baby crying before the door opened. A thin, dark woman with a straw hat entered. "I don't know what's wrong with him, doctor."

He took the card from the woman. "Sit down Miss . . . Berton."

"De baby cry all de time."

"How old's the child?"

"Six months, I reckon. Come during planting."

"Who delivered the child?"

"Widow Sanders done it."

"No doctor?"

"No suh. Couldn't afford no doctor. Had him at home."

"Don't you have any more clothes for him?" Jacob placed the baby on the examination table. "It's too cold for just a night shirt."

"Same thing all de the rest of us Bertons got by wid."

Jacob watched the long black fingers carefully unbotton the frail garment from the remarkably strong child. The black-skinned woman was handsome with her thick, curly hair brushed back and tied. He admired her high cheekbones. She appeared to be in her teens.

"Is this your first child?" He looked at her attractive body with a deep longing and admiration for a woman who appeared to be of largely African extraction. He feared the answer she might give, for her answer would mean that within a few short years she would look exactly like Mrs. Jackson. The woman's breasts that now had an easy upturn would soon hang like lifeless sacks.

"My first," she said, looking at the child and smiling.

Her smile exposed a mouth of rotten teeth. Jacob let his eyes fall from her face. She would be bound to have calcium deficiency.

"Do you breast feed him?"

"Yes suh."

"You don't look strong enough."

"Sometimes my sister helps. She had a baby dat died."

"What else do you feed the child?"

"I chews up food at de table and gives it to him."

"I see his nails are clipped."

"I chewed dem off so as he won't cut hisself."

The child, despite all of the worldly forces conspiring against it, seemed robust and healthy. Jacob had seen the children of the middle class in worse physical condition because of lack of care. Like the woman who allowed the child's saliva to run into the creases of its little fat neck and start an infection because she hated to wash the baby. Or the lady who fed her child orange soda instead of the prescribed juice.

"Does the father help?"

"Much as he kin. He says soon as he gits a good enough job we goin' to marry."

"Do you work?"

"Yes suh."

"Where?"

"At the 'bacca warehouse."

"That's heavy work."

"All us colored folks kin get."

"You got to put more cover on this child. Hand me that pin. There. I'll be right back with something for the child."

Jacob left treatment room One and went back through a series of white, gold-handled doors to treatment room Two.

"Mr. Greer, have you ever had pains before?" Greer gripped the edge of the treatment table with both hands, raised his large head and said with thick-lipped movements of his mouth, "Couple years past started coughin' and thought I had consumption. The Doc told me it was jest a cold. He made me take off my shirt just like you done and poked 'round. Boy? How long you been a doctor?"

"Ten years, Mr. Greer, don't worry." Jacob took his blood and a urine sample. The man was a wonderful physical specimen but before long the hard work would tell; as his weight increased from eating bad food, his heart would strain under the heavy load of work and his stomach, liver and internal organs would soon rebel from his intense physical activity and poor food. From all indications the man had become what Jacob called a humanoid—a person whose total mind is concerned with avoiding pain and whenever possible experiencing intense physical pleasure or intense pleasurable visions such as the church, narcotics or TV can give.

Before leaving, Greer paid Jacob cash and placed his hand upon Jacob's shoulder. "I heard 'bout you before, Doc. People say you been talking dangerous. I just want you to know dat you're okay by me. I like your style. Any time you down by Water Street just ask for Greer."

Jacob was momentarily shocked. He had expected less from Mr. Greer. He couldn't thank Greer because he realized he was campaigning to satisfy his ambitions as well as serve the people. "Glad to meet you, Mr. Greer." He knew Greer was impressed by the use of the formal title "Mister" by a doctor to a laborer.

Greer's response had surprised him but it had also reaffirmed some of the things he'd been saying during his campaign about the ability of the people to choose those to govern themselves. Jacob's miscalculation of Greer as a man brought the same type of shocking correction as did his first discovery of his own diminishing eyesight after thirty years of good vision, or his discovery that there were persons younger than himself who were more mature than he. When he was finally forced to really look at Greer, Jacob realized that there was something corrupt within his own self that wanted exorcising.

He didn't know how long he'd stood hesitating with his hand on the phone before he finally picked it up and asked for the next patient to be shown in.

Sheslona Frailty led her children into the room. One seemed to have been crying and the other had a glum face.

"Jacob, I don't know what to do with these children. Children don't have the manners today they once had," the matronly little woman said.

They don't have the parents they once had either, Jacob thought. "How are you, Godfry?" he asked.

"Okay."

"What kind of an answer is that to give Doctor Blue?" Sheslona asked. "Say fine thank you, sir." She shook the silent boy's arm. A scowl replaced the pout on his face.

"How has school been, Godfry?" Jacob asked the child.

"They're both at the head of their class. Godfry, tell the doctor what you learned in school today." She let go of his arm and stepped back with her arms folded menacingly to watch him perform.

"The American form of democracy is republican government."

"That's not right," his sister scolded. "Democracy is an American form of republican government," the little girl firmly stated.

"That's wrong," Godfry said.

"What are you going to be when you grow up?" Jacob sympathized with Godfry who had to live with two women constantly pushing and pulling at him.

"He's going to be a doctor. Like Doctor Blue. Isn't that right, Godfry?"

"Is someone sick?"

"No, we just thought we'd get some shots and get checked up. Can't be too careful. Polio and the flu haven't been wiped out completely."

"Sit down and relax. Be right with you," Jacob said, leaving the room.

Back with Miss Berton and her baby who sat small and quiet on the white iron chair Jacob took up a note pad. "I'm going to write the name of a formula you can pick up at the drugstore for . . . "

"Everything you done for me is good, Doctor. But I reckon I'M goin' to have to bring up MY baby the same way MY momma raised ME."

"Please try . . . "

"What you talkin' about, Doctor, is money and I just ain't got it."

"Where do you live, Miss Berton?"

"Out in the rurals."

"Don't you have someone in your family you could stay with for a month? Somewhere warm where you could rest and eat? It's a miracle the child's lived this far. No sense taking any more chances . . . "

"Trouble is, everybody got ideas 'bout how to raise the boy. Everybody's talkin' about *should,* but I's the one who has to think 'bout *got to.* Everybody got notions 'bout my baby . . . 'bout payin' fer this visit."

"You take your time, honey. And here." He took the cash Greer had given him from his pocket and stuffed it into her hand. "Take care of that child. He may be our only hope."

"Thank you, Doctor. I was afraid to come here at first 'cause of all the talk. But folk told me you'd even help a person poor and miserable as me." As the woman left, carrying the child on her hips, he thought she moved with the quiet grace of a black angel. Jacob called Nurse Waters.

It wasn't until five that Jacob had a chance to sit down. He had a cup of coffee warmed over from breakfast in his study while examining his daily mail, separating the trash from the stuff to be read and filed or answered. By five-thirty he was in his car hurrying down U.S. 59. The wheel of the car, which required constant attention at 85 mph, gave him a comfortable sense of freedom. He'd agreed with Jesse to meet there at Tent City at six to speak about something or another he felt was urgent. He'd wanted to visit the colony of farmers who were being evicted because of their involvement in his campaign for some time. Before the campaign began they knew there would be attacks and repressions, but they hadn't planned for anything like hundreds of people losing their homes.

On the crowded six-o'clock sidewalks doll-like secretaries switched their for-sale tails out of downtown offices. Big-headed businessmen wrapped up their last deals of the day ("And don't forget, J.P., if there's anything I can ever do for you just let me know," Jacob heard a man say as he stopped for a light.) Large irritable crowds of immaculate maids and tired janitors grabbed bus rides. Savagely vigorous grade school students screamed and fought their way home. Bus drivers quarreled with other drivers, "Hey bud. Where'd you get your license?" Cooks at the swank restaurants walked out of their hot kitchens into the air to take a smoke before preparing for the after-dinner movie crowd. Commuters rode in car pools to the green suburbs. At the Southern Arms Hotel, lonely women with no money met lonely men with money. Jacob knew that soon moneyed women would leave spent men who would be without money. He shivered to watch the tight-black-dressed women walking about their mesdames like dogs on a leash, for once in his youth he had followed a prostitute home. He thought of the apartment of the buxom, raven-haired Chicago beauty as a nest of filth. In the middle of the filth, on a mattress on the floor where the act was to take place, lay a baby that had been left, God knows how long, unattended. He'd paid the woman and left despite her pleadings for him to stay.

He turned from from the highway to a county road that ran along the canal by the Mississippi River. He passed a sprawling ragged village of wood cabins and cadaver-gray corrugated metal shacks patched with mud stacked on the side of a slight slope. Further along the winding road in a swampy field were house trailers enveloped with vines. Clotheslines were strung between the trailers. When Jacob was young, he and other children had called the place Cracker Town. And the whites had called Camp Grove, his section of town, Nigger Town. Jesse said that Tent City was just a little beyond Cracker Town on the county road. As Jesse had said, over a hill he found a muddy field with tents clustered in one corner. Deep car tracks led from the road to the tents. He saw a couple of cars and Jesse's truck by the tents.

Jacob parked and tried to make his way to the tents without sinking to his ankles in mud. Electric lines were connected to a pole in the yard and ran into the tents, which had antennae poking up from them. Smoke curled from stovepipes sticking through asbestos-reinforced holes. Jacob was frightened as he walked toward the fourteen or fifteen tents with his shoes making sucking sounds in the soft ground. He was afraid to think of the nature of suffering he might find within the brown canvas. In the soft afternoon light he made out a couple of men pushing up the center pole of another tent. Several black children sat with eyes bright and faces alert in the tent doorways. A couple of the older ones held rifles.

"Doctor Blue," a little boy called, running toward him. Soon he was surrounded by anxious little faces.

"Make a speech."

"I'm a first-class leaflet handler . . . "

"You come to make us free?"

"Huh, Doctor."

Jacob laughed. He felt relieved. "Where's Jesse?" he asked. The children led him through a yard of squawking children to a tent. Jacob climbed onto the platform and swept back the tent flap revealing a naked light bulb dimly illuminating the place, a large woman seated in a rocking chair, Jesse and Curt standing near a trunk that had a short-wave radio crackling on it and a little pot-bellied stove.

"Jacob," Jesse shouted, shaking his hand. "This is Mrs. Rowe and this is Curt, who's going to help us poll-watch Monday." The largest piece of furniture in the tent was a poster bed made up with a fluffy spread neatly turned back. "Sit down," Jesse said, returning to the radio.

He sat on the bouncy bed.

"Won't you have something to eat?" Mrs. Rowe asked. A pot on the stove, smelling strongly of greens, boiled, lifting its lid and dropping it.

"Running fox, calling base." Jesse flicked the switch on a microphone he held near his mouth. "Come in base."

Everyone looked at the black box covered with switches and waited. The response finally came. "This is base, go ahead running fox."

"The snake doctor has arrived. Ten-four."

"Ten-four," the radio said.

"You keep a close tab on me."

"Just a necessary precaution, Doc."

Outside the noise of hammers pounding stakes and nails cracked in the cool air.

Turning from the radio back to Mrs. Rowe, Jacob said, "No thank you." He felt a deep humility having been offered a share of a sparse meal by a woman whose family had been evicted after two hundred years in one spot merely because they wanted to vote for him.

"You shore now?" the woman insisted in the manner proper for courteous country folk. She was bound to force him to share her food with him. He had been polite by not accepting the first time, but he realized he couldn't turn down the second offer without offending the woman.

Sitting on the edge of the bed eating succulent greens spiced with a little fatback and herbs, Jacob listened to Jesse's low voice methodically lay out the problem.

" . . . if we can't keep the people in the county, we'll lose. When people are evicted they've got to come to Tent City until we can build houses or their sacrifices will be for nothing."

"White folks own all the land," Mrs. Rowe said. "Once they needed us. Now they got machines to do the work."

"Jacob. We need you to spend some time out here because there's a lot of sickness," Jesse said.

"They could condemn the place or quarantine it," Curt said.

Everyone stared at the stove for a while and listened to the hammers pounding outside. "The boy over in the third tent's actin' strange," Mrs. Rowe said. "Can't seem to get out of bed."

"I'll take a look at him," Jacob said.

Mrs. Rowe handed him a piece of cornbread to sop up the juice from the greens. "Boy, you sure favor the Ricks family. You ain't no kin to the Ricks, is you?"

"I don't know," he said.

"You ain't never lived on the Nicholson plantation, has you?"

"When I was too small to remember much, people tell me I lived there."

"What's your paw's name?"

"I never knew him," Jacob said. "My maw is called Anne Blue."

"Oh Lawd," she shouted. "Me and your maw used to pick mountains o' cotton together. My we had a time down in dem woods at de church near the creek. We carried tons o' 'tater salad, chicken and yams down to dat church. It sho' was a shame 'bout your paw."

"What do you mean?" Jacob asked. By the sudden pained expression on Mrs. Rowe's face he realized he should have kept quiet and let her talk.

Then with a deep, heavy sadness in her voice she said, "If you don't know, honey, I ain't de one to tell you."

Jacob quietly waited for her to continue. He hoped the silence would intimidate her into speaking. He put the plate on the trunk and looked with questioning eyes into the silent face of the old lady in a black smock, rocking back and forth. It was then that memories of a childhood full of signs and prophecy came back to him. "He'll be a doctor or a lawyer," the preacher had told his mother one day in front of their house. People had unreservedly pointed at him and whispered behind his back.

His thoughts were interrupted by a boy's face in the door of the tent. "Ya'll better come," he said.

Jesse and Curt hurried through the tent flap. Jacob followed them out of the tent and then across the yard through the gluey mud. They ran around a couple of tents and came to the truck.

"Damn," Curt said.

Only a few supporting rib pieces stood where the planks forming the sides of the truck had been.

"What happened?" Jesse asked the youngster.

"People needed some dry firewood. Trees are too green. Dem boards'll make good kindling," said the little fellow in an oversized army jacket.

While Jesse tried to piece together the truck with some rope and rickle, Jacob and Curt went to the tent with the sick boy. In the dark enclosure he lay under the covers on the bed, his slight frame barely discernible from the pile of covers about him. The tent held a large bureau with a mirror on it. Next to the bureau sat a fellow cleaning a semi-automatic rifle.

"Hello, Doc." The fellow, whose stone face and blank, almost lifeless eyes were unmoving, snapped the lever back to clear the weapon and then, with a quick movement of his thumb and forefinger, he snapped the chamber closed and pulled the trigger. "Better look him over," he said, pulling the trigger guard down, sliding the black metal gears of the trigger mechanism out and carefully dismantling it on a handkerchief he'd spread on the bureau.

Jacob pulled the covers back. "How long's he had a fever?"

"Day or more."

While the fellow by the trunk pulled the lever and spring away from the rifle and the barrel fell away from the stock, leaving every piece of the machine open to his stroking handkerchief, Jacob examined the little boy. He found what, without the aid of a blood test, appeared to be hepatitis. And in addition to the liver disease, which could be attributed to sanitary conditions, Jacob found the child's feet cracked and bleeding from frost bite he'd gotten sleeping in the cabins without cover. The fellow in the corner cleaning the gun said they'd not had any trouble with the cold since moving into the tents —they were warmer than the shacks that had been their former homes. Before he left, Jacob shook hands with the gunman, who said his name was Jay Van and he was called J. V.

By the time Jacob left Tent City he had examined everyone and determined what he had known before he'd come, that they were in trouble and that disease could wipe them out at any moment. The area could be quarantined if the case of hepatitis spread and it became publicized. So Jacob set up rules about not exchanging articles of clothing or eating utensils with anyone living in the sick boy's tent. He'd have to come back up there Friday with vaccine. He also proposed that they dig a cesspool and build a well on high ground.

That, plus the use of lye and soap, would help solve some of the problems. But the most serious problem couldn't be solved by this kind of attention. Jacob was most deeply disturbed by the fact that there was no common viewpoint among the people about their direction or even what had happened to them. There was no common greeting or common words used which would indicate the existence of camaraderie. The physical problems would be solved, with God's help, but the spiritual problems might be their undoing.

3

Leah

"I DON'T KNOW WHY some people act like that," Leah said, gossiping with the maid. "It's disgraceful, Jeanne. Why does she keep having children if she can't take care of them?"

"Don't know no better, I guess," Jeanne said straightening her lap-sized black apron.

"Honey, did you hear about Mrs. Jones?"

Jeanne shook her head as she turned the flame off under the meat.

"A friend of Jacob's who's a lawyer told me she sent her three children to her husband's—they're separated, you know. He sent them back and she called the police and had him arrested."

"No," Jeanne said in mock surprise.

"That's right and then she sent the kids back to his place in a cab alone. Why the oldest one's only twelve."

"She ought to be whipped, child. Tina Moore told me the Gittens can't find a place to stay. Their daughter has a baby and they're sleeping in tents."

"Disgraceful," Leah said.

"Do you want me to take something up to your mother, dear?"

"No, I'll take something up to her on my way up to my room. I've got to get ready."

As Leah scraped some pieces of rabbit and vegetables onto a plate, Jeanne sat on a kitchen stool and started reading the *Courier*. An ad caught her eye.

It read:

> Wherever you live, I have a special blessing for you. I can help you to be successful in all walks of life. If you live in New York State, California, Ohio, Pennsylvania, Washington, D. C., Massachusetts, Connecticut or Michigan I have a special Saturday blessing from the Lord for you. In any other state try my weekly two-for-one blessing rate good only during this month.
>
> Let me send you four prospective numbers as news, information and socio-statistical data, not to be construed in any way as gambling.
>
> So many people have been swindled and lied to.
>
> I will destroy enemies. Give protection, make them bow to you, return husbands, stop wives from chattering, return stolen goods, cure bronchitis, make him do anything you say if you only send money quickly to me.

Try lucky lode stones ...... $2.00 a pair
First Luck Brand incense .. $1.00
Beau Catcher fragrance $2.00
Success Brand oil, root
and luck coin $2.00

Scriptures and special financial message of Del are
sent to you three hours after we receive your word by
telegram, air freight, express greyhound or trailway.

This is for the ones who have been everywhere and
tried everything. Have no fear because I, Rev. K. L.
Conklin, is here. God's personal blessing will be yours.
I will analyze your problems from the cradle to the
grave.

ONE WAY, ONE DAY, ONE PHONE CALL WILL CONVINCE
YOU.

For fast, quick, efficient action call me.

If it's voodooration, conjuration or constipation let
me do the conjuring for you.

I also cure those embarassing "natures" problems.

WAMSAIDE K. L. Conklin
Box 33
Cape Rondebosh
South Africa.

Please indicate in your letter whether you want 24,
48 or 72 hour deliverance.

A succulent aroma rose from the rabbit dinner on the stove.
Salad vegetables lay on serving dishes. Soft patches of day's last
light sifted through the lace curtains giving the kitchen a hazy
glow. In the dining room Leah could see the silverware and
napkins in place, gray pussy willow sprigs decorating the center
of the table and tall crystal glasses holding foggy, tepid water.

With a tray of food, water, and a knife and fork, Leah left
the warm kitchen and climbed the back stairway to a dimly lit

sitting room. As her eyes accustomed themselves to the gloom, she could see the room's detail: drapes, stuffed velvet-covered chairs of deep gold and scarlet red, grandfather and cuckoo clocks, dusty leather-bound books, a thick Persian carpet with design obscured by age. A four-foot-tall vase in one corner of the room that held a few cattails added a musky odor to the room. Porcelain maids with water cans, figurines of lackeys and piles of glass ash trays crowded the lamp tables. A shaft of light penetrating a velvet window curtain bustled with specks of dust and slashed the room in two from the crack in the curtain across the ceiling to the lower part of the opposite wall where it illuminated the faint flower pattern of the wallpaper. Barely visible in one corner of the room was a walnut-faced old woman wrapped in a shawl.

"Here we come, Momma Blue. Time for dinner, dear," Leah said handing the old woman the plate.

"You didn't have to bring it up."

"I was on my way to my room and I thought you might enjoy eating up here. You like this room so much."

"I was hoping to eat with you folk. Wanted to talk to Reverend Grace."

"But it's so tiring for you, Momma." Leah walked softly to the window and peeked from behind the curtains to stare at autumn leaves trembling in the wind. From the darkening wood beyond the garden, sprays of bats leaped into the sky and careened toward the house. She trembled at the sight of a world standing tiptoe on the verge of winter. A few pumpkins dotted the brown earth, corn husks were gathered into neat piles and the earth was bathed in deep browns and reds by the sinking sun. "Gettin' dark," the old wrinkled woman whispered and then returned to her meal and resumed the noise of her loose dentures.

Leah rushed from the room in fear of the musky death smell that always surrounded the old woman, not wanting to talk; for what do the aged talk about but the deaths they have lived to see, the lives they have survived and the death they daily face.

Leah knew the story of the woman's life; she had worked from sunup to sunset since she could remember and Leah despaired to hear of the old woman's labors or of the church—after all what possibly could an old black woman have to say to her, the young wife of an enterprising doctor? And of all things, the old woman seemed to be dissatisfied with her son's marriage. The old lady was demanding of Jacob and herself some mysterious, unnamable thing. The old woman's control over Jacob was almost sinister, Leah had decided.

In the bathroom Leah pulled off her padded bra, wiggled out of her girdle and slowly laved her corpulent body, exploring all the creases and folds of flesh with the cloth.

Sitting before the dressing table mirror she looked at her own form in the faded yellow light of the lamp. She held the folds of fat that girdled her waist in her hands. After pulling a comb through her stiff black hair she removed it and placed the wig carefully on a wig stand. Grown tired of black hair, she'd have to dye it red or maybe put a silver streak in it adding a bit of dignity befitting her age.

On her way back to the kitchen she looked in on Momma Blue. The old woman gently rocked her body, staring at faceless clocks and listening to their tricky ticking till light faded from the last bluff that floated on the horizon somewhere above Louisiana. As Leah picked up her plate of chewed-over food, she switched on a table lamp and flipped through a black bound bible. Hesitating, she studied the red edges of the pages and the gold margin. The edge was the color of aging blood and the margin had the tinge of yellow Mississippi wastelands; inside the print was large, black and cruelly twisted gothic type. Her lips moved as her eyes followed her finger across the page. She didn't notice Leah take the plate.

"Are you coming down to have some coffee with us?" Leah whispered.

Momma Blue looked up and said, "I may. If'n you ain't ashamed to have me meet your company."

"Don't say that, Momma Blue."

"Don't," the old lady shrugged her shoulders as Leah tried to place her hand on her shoulder.

The sound of the last horseshoe clinked in the clear night air signaling the end of a game in back of the Blue house. Neighborhood folk had appropriated the land and dug a pit, for people in Camp Grove took their horsehoes seriously. Jacob thought it was funny and encouraged the men and boys, but Leah thought it was outrageous and caused ugly bare places in the yard she tried so hard to keep green.

"Everybody's here except Mr. Blue and Mr. Frailty and Shessy," Jeanne announced when Leah stepped into the kitchen.

"Shessy made a good catch when she hooked onto John," Leah said. "It's taken them a long time, but it looks like their hard work's going to pay off."

"You know *how* he made his money, don't you?" Jeanne carefully studied Leah's expression for some indication that Leah's curiosity would encourage her to continue a dangerous line of talk.

"I *thought* he made his money in the funeral business."

"No, not at all. Jacob probably told you that. Men can't see the nose on their faces. *Numbers*, baby."

"How do you know?"

"This little momma's been around."

"That's just gossip," Leah said in a tone indicating insult and a close of the subject, at least until her imagination once more pricked her.

4

Judge Clayton Tips the Scales of Justice

"WAY DOWN SOUTH in the land of cotton, old times there are n'er forgotten. Look away, look away, look away, Dixieland. Oh, I wish I was in Dixie, away, away. Oh, to live and die in Dixie. That's where the darkies play," Judge Marshall Clayton sang in his chamber. He'd make this a short day. He'd end the afternoon session early and go to pick up Laura, eat and then get on over to Bernard's. He had a lot to say to Bernard. The way he was kicking niggers and even poor white folk off the land was drawing the attention of Washington. He'd have to warn him to let things cool down a while.

There was something wrong. The moment Marshall Clayton walked into the courtroom for the afternoon session he sensed something radically different in the air, something that he didn't like. But he couldn't put his finger on it to save his life.

"Oh, I wish I was in Dixie" kept going through his head.

"All rise. Hear ye. Hear ye. Hear ye. The honorable court of the town of Matchez is now in session."

As he sat, the vaultlike room rustled with the noises of a hundred persons taking their seats. Clayton straightened his robe, looked over the docket and then raised his head to look out over the bench to the courtroom.

Mostly colored, he thought. He turned his white-haired, white-faced head to the prisoner's bench. Most, again, were black.

Notable among the prisoners were a white couple who sat arm-in-arm like children. The woman with her finger in her mouth and the man with his strawlike hair disheveled, she shared the red glow of alcoholics. White trash, Clayton thought. He would find them guilty of drunken and possibly disorderly conduct and resisting arrest and give them ten days or ten dollars.

"Let's git going," Clayton urged the prosecutor.

A sulking man who Clayton couldn't help but think looked like the colored fellow he played with as a child came from the prisoners dock with cap in hand and joined a worried woman before the bench. Of all things, the boy brought back memories of living around a smoky coal stove. The woman in clothes worn thin by constant washing, wrung her large rough black hands. The palms were light brown. They were the firm sort of hands that hold white children on the toilet, feed a hungry boy, spank him and cover him in bed with blankets. He stared down at the woman's large breasts as they heaved beneath her flowered dress.

The bailiff walked up to the microphone and raised it to the level of the prosecutor's mouth. Clayton remembered when the bailiff's mother had begged him to find a job for her son after he'd flunked out of school.

"This here boy's charged with disorderly conduct, your honor," the prosecutor said. "Resisted arrest and tried to strike an officer."

Clayton leaned over the bench to stare into the boy's guilt-filled, red eyes. With sympathy, to the woman, he said, "When they get drunk they can outfight, outcurse and outrun anybody in the world." He watched the eyes of the hundred Negroes in the court smile as he smiled. Then Clayton and over two hundred eyes looked sternly at the young man and said, "Your attitude disturbs me. Do you work?"

"No sir," he said.

"Speak up. Right into the mike," the prosecutor snapped.

"What do they call you, boy?" Clayton wanted urgently to get rid of the case, but felt that only by taking proper time with the boy would justice be done to the seriousness of his office.

"They call me Rog."

"That'll be thirty-five dollars fine."

A rumble of voices swept through the courtroom. He banged the gavel. The impertinence of the people in the courtroom bothered him. That's what he'd sensed when he'd first walked in. It was the fault of the higher courts and the type of decisions they were handing down. He wouldn't go so far as to say they were communistic, but the higher courts were handing down decisions that could only lead to anarchy.

"Quiet or I'll clear the courtroom. I don't know why but you're gitting off light," he told the boy. "Only time will tell."

The woman cried out, "Thank you, your honor. Thank you."

"You're his wife, I suppose?"

"Yes sir."

"That boy's kind of old to be cutting up like that." The colored fellow appeared to be in his thirties. It was remarkable how fast Matchez Negroes ran down after thirty. Men couldn't work for illness and the women weren't good for nothin' no more after thirty.

The woman closed her mouth up tight and looked at him the way his dogs did at times when he whipped them, full of confused love and hate.

"You didn't drink any of that wine Rog drank, did you?" The court laughed. Clayton banged his gavel.

"Oh no, your honor," the woman said.

Clayton suddenly felt at ease and in complete control of his courtroom. The wheels of justice were oiled and moving quickly forward.

"You can pay at the clerk's office." The bailiff led the couple away. "Call the next case."

"Mr. Wilson was just out in the hall making a call, your honor," Braden, the prosecutor, said. The bailiff headed out the courtroom door looking for Wilson.

Clayton leaned back in his soft cushioned chair and asked Braden, "You think the Braves will whip the Bears again?"

Glad for a moment's break in the tense courtroom procedure, Braden smiled and said, "If Grey is playing, yes. If he's still out with a sprained leg, no."

Shortly the bailiff came back with a smart looking man following him. Clayton noted the impeccable dress of the fellow approaching the bench. What could he have done? He looked down to his notes. *Illegal possession of drugs.* He was a real slicker—the kind that would hang around a school and sell drugs to high school students. He wondered who his lawyer might be?

The defendant—one of those thin, habitually nervous sorts—

walked to the bench. His black hair was pasted down—like the Italians' who ran the cafe—to his small head. "I don't think there's any need for a trial, your honor," he said. "The drugs are prescription. But if you think there are grounds for a trial, I want a little time to contact my lawyer and prepare my defense."

"I suppose you can substantiate that?" Clayton said.

"Yes sir."

"Is Officer Hurst here?" On the docket Hurst was listed as the arresting officer. Hurst slowly walked to the bench, his gait full of the slothful arrogance Clayton hated to see in poor whites. "This man says he can prove his drugs are prescription. If he can prove that to your satisfaction will you drop the charges?"

"Reckon so. You come to see me at my office tomorrow with your prescription or a doctor's statement, you hear?"

"Yes sir," Wilson said.

As Wilson walked away Clayton thought of a maxim old Judge Rhone had once told him: "Never underestimate the lowest white man. Some day he'll be able to help you with his franchise or his inheritance." He didn't understand his old teacher at first, but following that sagacious advice had paid off. He smiled to himself thinking, yes, you could say I've been paid off many times over. No matter how you played it the name of the game was the same.

"This here boy had whiskey what didn't have taxes paid on it," Braden said, presenting his next case.

What the hell, Clayton thought. This is a dry state. Why should the police collect taxes on illegal whiskey? Clayton watched Hurst's hand rise up his pants leg to the place where his gun was holstered. Fondling a gun was one of those habits of the police that secretly infuriated Clayton, for it was, to him, as annoying as trying to talk to a man while he picked balls of hair from his ass.

"How do you plead?"

"Innocent, your honor. Can I ask you a question?" the fellow said sassily.

Clayton leaned forward.

"When can I make a phone call to let my family know where I am?"

Clayton didn't like the attitude of the accused one bit. Everything about this case bothered him. The accused, a dark-skinned man with shirttails out, looked sultrily about the room. According to the police report on the fellow, he had a long record. From his attitude, he didn't seem to care about his fate. Maybe if he was bound over to the grand jury and cooled his heels in prison for a while he'd think more seriously of the matter. How could you try someone who didn't seem to care about the law?

"Bound over to the grand jury. Bond set at five hundred dollars."

The black man was led away.

Again there was an uncommon undercurrent in the court. Pockets of silence hid within the noises of the people and there was whispering underneath the silence. This was an unlucky day for him. He should have stayed at home, for it was on that day, ten years previously, that his mother had died. She had remained beautiful to the last and ignored his existence to the last. She had refused to let him call her mother. Instead he'd called her Aunt Laura. He'd never known why until he found the date of her marriage. He was born six months after his mother's wedding. Why hadn't his mother, like any decent white woman, gotten an abortion? But he, no more than any man, could affect the course of life before his own manhood.

Clayton whispered to the bailiff who repeated to the courtroom the words, "The court will be adjourned for ten minutes."

He hurried through the mahagony door to his chambers. Ensconced in his tiny closet-sized bathroom, the pain of elimination convinced him he would have to endure another operation for piles. He looked at the red blood in the commode swirling down with the water that would soon be in the Mississippi River. He washed his hands at the basin and primly combed his hair. In his office he pulled a cut-glass bottle from his desk and poured out a jigger of bourbon. After downing the rough-tasting liquor he placed a piece of Sen-Sen on his tongue.

Clayton reentered the court about the time the warmth of the liquor spread over his whole body.

"All stand," the bailiff chanted.

And when Clayton carefully sat down, everyone else in the court sat. He was slightly dizzy with liquor and his piles itched.

"How do you plead to these charges?" he asked a dried-up old gal before him.

"Not guilty, your honor," she said with a husky voice.

A laborer, if his clothes were any indication of his occupation, walked to the mike. The prosecutor asked, "Tell the court what happened, Sam."

"Me and this 'oman had a couple o' drinks. I spent the night with her and when I woke up my wallet was gone."

"Any other witnesses, Colonel Braden?"

"No sir."

"You got anything to say?" Clayton leaned forward on his elbows to emphasize the gravity of the situation. How did these people live? he wondered. Cutting, lying, stealing, whoring.

"I went out with that man. We drank and he wanted to go to bed. But when he told me what he wanted to do in bed I told him I didn't go that way. Then he said he wouldn't pay 'cause I wouldn't do somethin' unnatural . . . "

Bang. Bang. Clayton pounded for order. After all a man, whether he were white or black, had a right to feel safe when he was doing a little catting.

"Twenty-seven-dollar fine for drinking," Clayton sputtered above the courtroom noise.

The woman, to Clayton's utter dismay, switched her skinny ass out the prisoner's docket into the lock-up. As she disappeared, trailed by a manly-looking police matron, he thought that by all rights he should fine the hussy for contempt.

Petty thieves, brawlers and drunks received of grace and punishment according to his feelings, Clayton adjourned court for the day. The cool, air-conditioned and book-lined room, smelling of the musk of old Mississippi code books, always helped him to relax. He went to the desk and pulled out the liquor and took another nip to improve his appetite.

The Southern Insurance Commissioners' meeting was going on in a local hotel. He hadn't time to attend, but hoped to see Ed and Jack from the Jackson comptroller's office afterward at the Nicholson's party. He was anxious to speak to them about an idea he had about developing Matchez. Everyone was trying to figure how to stimulate economic activity, but no one would listen to his simple, but effective plan. His idea was to bring horse racing to Matchez. Horse racing would generate a lot of tourism and movement that would be good for retail business and service industries. Matchez folk could show even Kentucky folk a thing or two about horse racing. So many people already raised horses for fox hunts that they would be able to enter in races for the fun of it all.

He hung his black robe on a clothes tree, slipped on his jacket and exited through the main office saying goodbye to the clerks and the guard.

"Evening paper says the stock market's recovered," the old chief clerk of the court told him.

"I told you. There ain't nothin' in the world more stable than the American dollar."

Devaluation of the pound had scared a lot of people into buying gold and selling stock, but he had remained steadfast.

"Way down south in the land of cotton, old times there are n'er forgotten, look away, look away, look away, Dixieland," Clayton sang, driving his old black Cadillac toward the Hofstra Training School for Girls. He thought of his young niece with her saucer shock-sheen eyes and her suave suede boots, of her swinging walk, her monkey face and flopping hair. She was every bit a part of the exciting ugliness Clayton found in the younger generation. She was like one of those improbably impudent teen-agers who slung their behinds around on the TV programs. He would pick Laura up and drive her to his home to enjoy a specially prepared meal of creole shrimp. He held the hope that he could convince her to accompany him to the meeting later in the evening at Bernard Nicholson's place. She always was a lively little piece to have on his arm at a party.

Unhappily, she was the image of Rose. Laura's mother, his sister, had married at quite a young age a man of low station in life, discrediting herself in many people's eyes. Rose, who took after their mother's family, as he, thank God, took after their father's, had achieved national notoriety as a collector of antique furniture. Father's family had a long, tiresome geneal-ogy, which Clayton'd often read in the Matchez library, going back to the jails of England. Rose had married, as many women do, because she was curious. It seemed only natural that her daughter would turn out a coquette. When Rose died and her husband ran off to Europe, Clayton was left with the girl. He thanked God for Mrs. Wisner, head of Hofstra, who'd taken special interest in the direction of Laura's life.

During the blinding pace of Thanksgiving through Christ-mas, Mrs. Wisner had encouraged Laura to give presents to the poor. Each year there was a touching scene around the tree in the main hall where Laura handed out the toys, trucks and model guns to wide-eyed boys and golden-haired dolls to the little black girls. This was good, for he believed that as the men of a race should know the value of aggression, the women should know the value of charity.

The white gravel of Hofstra school was shaded by large moss-covered trees fuzzy gray with the omnipresent rotting growth. As Clayton gave the keys to his car to an attendant to park he couldn't help but think of the days of his youth when Hofstra had been the home of the Lees and the center for entertainment of the town's leading families and their important guests. It was at a ball at the Lee's that Rose, his sister, had met her husband, a common school teacher. God rest her soul, Rose's marriage had only been a marriage in name, for although Rose and Edward had lived under the same roof, they had had neither the élan nor the sexual liberties characteristic of married people. Laura was, so to speak, a mistake. Laura's beauty proved to Clayton his theory that behind all beauty there was eternal sadness.

As Clayton crossed the porticoed porch he hoped he wouldn't meet any of the instructors at the school who would deem it their duty to engage him in long and meaningless conversations on questions neither of them knew anything about but had the good taste to have opinions on—a habit of the cultured. Luckily the route to Ethel Wisner's office was clear and he found the virtuous lady busy at her desk.

"What's happening to the stock market?" Ethel said, embracing him.

"Just a little peaked. The Federal Reserve gave it a shot in the arm today and it's bounced back."

"Do you think Jacob Blue has a chance to win the race for Congress?" she asked, trying to make small talk.

He gave the proper reply. "Hell no, no nigger's represented Mississippi in Congress since the ruinous reconstruction during what my grandfather called the slight misunderstanding between brothers, and one never will again." But he knew that a whole heap of Negroes had been registered through the efforts of the Justice Department and rights agitators and that Blue might actually win unless the proper precautions were taken. But how can you tell a woman that?

"I just don't know what this state is coming to," she said, "allowing a nigra to become a serious contender for such a high office."

"Don't worry none about it. There's still some men in this state."

"I have something very serious to talk to you about." She dutifully poured Clayton a drink from her private stock. Ethel knew his tastes well. She was patient until he, after twirling the drink around in the glass as was his habit, downed the shot of bourbon and was ready, then, to discuss any matter. "You know that I regard your niece as more than a student. Ever since she came heah I've treated her as one of the family and have actually gone out of mah way to understand her as a person, no matter what difficulties she presented."

"You've done a remarkable job. And Ah know she's hard to handle. On some ways she takes after my side of the family. Why when I was her age, many times the only way Auntie could control me was to have the Sheriff lock me up. Hurt my pride more than anything else," he said contritely.

Ethel thrust a lavender-colored note toward him. "I found this letter in her room." He straightened the crushed paper and read among the patterns of the folds, "Yes. I like modeling for you. When can I do it again?" Black-cloaked thoughts ran like night horsemen through his mind. The letter itself was not as incriminating as the questions it probably answered.

"Modeling?" Clayton asked.

"For the art instructor."

"Schneider?"

"Schneider. Herr Schneider, the students call him," the tired, and, at that moment, especially gaunt-looking woman said. Why he'd be damned if Ethel Wisner didn't look like the drawn and withered women out in Cracker Town. That particularly unflattering thought wouldn't unstick itself from his mind. He imagined that her stiff business suit was made of crocus sacks.

So, Schneider was behind all this. A man kicked out of the State School because his work was criticized by local politicos, fools, who considered themselves art critics. But they hadn't looked at the art. He knew John Cableton, one of those chiefly responsible for Schneider's dismissal, and he was less an art critic than his cook. Cableton had seen rather unflattering political messages in the professor's paintings. Consequently many in the town accused Schneider of having been sired by a Negro female dog and a select few townspeople gossiped that Schneider liked to smell women's underclothes and found easy access to such garments at his present place of employment. Schneider was foolish not to do something about such gossip and since he hadn't, he was, in fact, either guilty or not a man for a man stuck up for what he stood for!

"I'll speak to the girl," he lied. The best thing to do in this case would be to remain silent. Schneider would be quietly dismissed and this time he would have to leave town. Excited, he choked on his drink and Ethel gave him a few pats on the back. "You . . . cough . . . speak to Schneider . . . cough . . . about opportunities in the East."

There burned in his heart a fearful warm glow. Laura was undoubtedly discovering how to love herself. She wanted to be painted. Soon some man would teach her to love the beauty of another. She would be screwed. He choked again. Ethel wasn't helping at all. "Damn it," he said. "Hit me hard if you want to help . . . cough, choke . . . burp. That's it." Clayton lay back on a tortured-looking piece of furniture of early American design and looked with expectancy toward the dark hallway.

"Ça va?" Laura asked.

"Toute va bien, mademoiselle," he said rising and performing a funny little bow.

Laura, the image of his sister, chattered like one of those lovely tropical birds. "There's a lovely pair of gloves downtown. Divine. I want you to buy them for me, Uncle. I won't let anyone else buy them for me. I'll wear them to graduation." Clayton could rarely think of a thing to say to the girl that might interest her. His face reddened and his color grew hot as the heat of the day became unbearable.

Laura, Clayton noticed, was gaining weight in her cheeks and around her breasts and hips. She was no longer the wild tomboy who burned barns and stole his liquor for fun and who outran, outate, and outlied men twice her age. As they hugged she kissed him on both cheeks. Her perfume smelled like candy. In that respect she had the taste of an infant. But her candy smell was better—much better—than the harsh smell of Ethel.

He struggled to keep the redhead from kissing him on his bald spot; one of her many annoying habits.

When they had their car brought around front, Laura insisted upon driving. The news commentator on the car radio was speaking of some unpleasantry and he moved the dial. News was on all the stations. Some young fellow, trying to talk with authority, said, "You have not heard 'Hail to the Chief' until you have heard it played by men in fatigues and steel helmets. This is the first president since Lincoln to go into a war zone to shake hands with the troops and eat with them . . . "

"They were both trying to free niggers," Clayton said.

Keeping her eye on the road Laura said, "I don't understand you. You old people are so bitter."

"I'm quite sure, young lady, that the wisdom of my age has some little thing it can afford to give your youthful and blissful ignorance."

As they stopped for a light Laura laughed and lightly touched his head. He drew back angrily. She was just like her mother, he decided. For the briefest second Clayton lapsed into a daydream where Laura wandered about barefoot in a wood, hunting for him. But he was invisible to her and she kept walking past him.

"Da, da, da, dadadada," Laura sang with a record on the radio, snapping her fingers in utter disrespect and shaking her head and shoulders about like a palsied person. Clayton glanced at her legs. They were moving too. Remarkable that such a beautiful child was on the way to ruin.

The light changed and the acceleration of the car pushed him back in the seat.

It was the same red hair lightly tossed up on her head, on that keen face with perfect Nordic features but with a hint of the darker Southern European races about the eyes and lips that had been the downfall of her mother, and Laura, like her mother, was conscious of her beauty and used it to gain whatever she could. Hopefully, she, unlike Rose, would be kept in schools and traveling abroad with responsible companions until the right match could be arranged. He would like to see her hooked up to a Beufort, a Hunt or even a Nelson and if Bernard Nicholson wasn't such a young devil, he would make a smart match. His family didn't have a name going back hundreds of years, but had during the past century gained money; a lot of money.

"Uncie," Laura said. "I met the most heavenly boy down at the library today."

"What was his name?"

"Ernest Ramsey. He's working at the rocket base they're building over near the coast. He just came down from Huntsville. He knew Brig Anderson. Says they studied aeronautics together at Old Miss. Ernest told me all about it. He says he studies how rockets act that are still in the atmosphere, but that he's really interested in space study. I hope I'll see him at the library every day."

"I hope you get some work done while you're there. Invite him over some time."

"Oh, no."

"What?"

"He's got long blond hair and loves to talk girl talk. He's just a silly boy."

The judge was at a loss for words and swelled up inside. Out of the corner of his eye he noticed her head bouncing in time with the car radio music.

"What is the God-awful sound on the radio?" he asked her, trying to break into her consciousness and realizing that her mind was in tune with the music.

" 'The Funky Momma Blues,' " she said.

He was afraid to ask her what that might mean.

The dinner went more smoothly than Clayton had hoped. Afterwards he caught a nap while Laura joined one of her best friends in a phone chat. The meal had been eaten with wine and after dinner there was cognac. Clayton reflected in recline upon his bed with an amiable glow in his body that the only unpleasantry had been Laura's statement that she hoped Jacob Blue won his campaign and he'd been forced to explain, with some firmness, that a black Congressman would not only be against tradition and good taste, but against the intentions of God. She seemed sobered by his deeply felt comments.

After showering, Clayton powdered his patchy, puffy, flaccid flesh until it was an even smooth white from his feet to his face. He pulled on a pair of silk shorts and although the season was late he wore his white suit and white shoes. It was cold and snowing in Chicago when he'd flown there the week before for a conference called by the Legion, but there were still many sunny days left before winter blasted Mississippi.

Alone in his study he walked to the bar to fix a gin and tonic. He fumbled through his billfold to make sure he had enough pocket money. One hundred dollars ought to do the job. Propitiously studying the picture above his desk, Clayton stood in the middle of the floor, legs apart, sipping the gin. Were we wrong? he asked, staring at the mural of slaves, plantation owners and southern belles on the wall above the books.

Suddenly remembering a part of his toilet he'd overlooked, he ran into the bedroom, opened his shirt and squirted vapor from a can of deodorant into his armpits. The cool spray felt as delicious as the pine scent smelled. He massaged hand lotion into his palms. The aroma of specially imported Portuguese soap he'd discovered while traveling on the continent hung about his body.

Clayton returned to the study and stared at the mural. My malicious fathers, he thought, maliciously pursued their unholy business of traffic in Congolese and Guinean souls and I, a good son, will respectfully carry on my father's faith.

His old man was a hell of a fucker and his grandfather before him.

Hell no. If it wasn't for slavery I wouldn't be where I now stand, he thought. The whole nation, thanks to the old fuckers, has flowered.

In the front parlor he found a note in the familiar scrawl of the elusive Miss of his life saying he could find her at the Nicholson's. She'd taken a cab after waiting as long as she could, the cursive letters said.

In his big blue Buick he wound through the dust-filled streets under a canopy of blazing trees touched by the late autumn whose leaves rustled above the car like a sea of plants whipped up by the wind. He wound up the drive of Nicholson's house and parked at the front door, leaving his keys for the boy. He had to talk business with young Nicholson. There was the matter of the re-zoning of some land Bernard had his eye on and then the trouble with the Justice Department. It was through keeping his eyes open that he stayed in office. Through his connections his nomination was always assured; nomination by the Party being as good as winning an election. A lot of men on the Party central committee owed him favors, not the least of whom was Sam Nicholson, the big small-town banker. Since Clayton had taken office years ago, the bounty of Matchez had overflowed, bringing upon him the weight and dignity of office that almost made him cry and especially saddened him when he watched Negroes grabbing their caps from their heads as he drove past. They didn't understand what a heavy burden office-holding was, how much the public required of their public servants. As he entered the house the band struck up Dixie and a Negro with a microphone announced him. He quickly made his way among the guests and waiters who offered him drinks and tidbits on trays. He was looking for Sam or Bernard.

5

John Frailty

JOHN FRAILTY SHOWERED with odorless soap, for he couldn't afford to offend anyone that evening, nor could he seem in any way unusual. He was a man whose every gesture bespoke his constant compromise with life and the liberal reward he'd received from the authorities for that compromise. Coming baby-clean from the shower he noticed his wife, Shessy, had lain out his continental-cut suit. That would be a horrible mistake for although he would wear his thin-soled tapered Italian shoes a hippy-looking suit would be too adventuresome and not show due respect.

He wrapped a hot towel around his neck during his hair treatment and shave. His hair—wet from the shower—needed grease or it would dry unruly with frizzles and kinks. He poked his finger in a jar of Duke and worked a gob of it into his hair. A stiff brush plastered it down.

"Too much luv, too much luv, nothin' kills a nigger like too much luv . . . " he sang. He hated shaving and was convinced that his stiff bristly beard came from his early use of a safety razor rather than an automatic shaver. But automatics hadn't been perfected in his day. He'd been growing a neat little moustache, cultivating it for the women, but that had to go because it might offend the white folks he would see later in the evening after dinner at Jacob's. He jerked as he cut it off, as though he'd cut a living part of his body, but laughed when he realized what a small concession that was compared to what he had to lose if he'd worn it out of some abstract sense of manhood. Frailty, as usual, had a little smile on his face. A smile other people couldn't stand.

He pulled a double-breasted pin-striped blue business suit from his wardrobe and then checked his shirt collar to see if the stays were in place. "Shessy, where are my collar stays?"

Sheslona, the worried little dumpy woman who lived with him as his wife, fretted about the tray on Frailty's dresser, found the stays and quietly disappeared again. She wore a shapeless, colorless dress and was the type woman who would leave no impression upon anyone's mind who might meet her. She was going to a PTA meeting and wouldn't accompany him on his regular weekly visit to Jacob's.

Frailty took the shoe trees from his shoes. Shessy had brushed them the night before. He pulled his black socks high up onto his calves and looked for his garters—if there was one thing that could make him uncomfortable it was socks slipping down in his shoes so that when he crossed his legs his pants rode up making it appear that he were sockless. "Where's my garters?" he screamed. He couldn't be late. Shessy, who was sure and staid, but too damn slow as far as he was concerned, came back into the bedroom and found the garters. "Tonight I'll drive the Buick. You can have the Cadi to go over to the school and take the baby-sitter home later."

Standing in front of his house, Frailty buttoned his suit against the wind, which carried silk milkweed on its breath and shook trees that scratched the windowpane of his house. Down Electric Avenue at Jacob's place on the corner of Mangrum, Frailty saw a number of cars, indicating that the other guests had arrived. He jumped into his old Buick and rolled the couple of blocks to Jacob's.

Confidently tucking his briefcase under his short arms, Frailty walked across the porch, hesitating to touch with the tips of his fingers the head of a whitewashed clay figure in shackles. The clay man had strained against his chains a long time. A network of cracks and the soft shadow of green mold covered the total form.

Jeanne showed him into the study where he found Grace and Strop. "Sorry I'm late but I had to go home and clean up after a series of meetings downtown."

"Did you attend the National Association of Negro Markets?" Grace asked.

"Yes. At the Hotel Commodore," he confirmed, proud to be able to say that a Negro organization had held a meeting at a hotel that was all white just a year before.

6

Eating at the Table of Despair

JACOB ENTERED THE STUDY dressed in white and black tweed, holding a large tomcat in his arms. The cat, afraid of the visitors, squirmed from Jacob's grip and ran out of the room. Jacob greeted Frailty, Strop and Grace and settled back in his armchair. Strop and Grace sat on the couch and Frailty sat in a stiff-backed chair near the desk where he rested his briefcase. They drank a good blend of whiskey and nibbled bits of cheese and meat while speaking around important issues in a guarded way but trying most of all to make conversation about things of no vital interest.

Jacob rather liked Grace, the overstuffed high-yellow preacher. He had sublimely mastered his field. He could use anthropology, sociology or epistemology as well as theology to prove anything that might benefit him. Grace saw the church as, unhappily, the strongest organization that he, as a black man, would ever be a part of. At one point in Jacob's campaign, when deacons and bishops in the church had opposed his nomination, Grace had been central in organizing support for him and bringing him the most essential support of the AME-Zion church.

Strop was enjoyable when he was drunk but extremely dangerous when sober. Jacob shuddered to think of what the man taught pupils at Carver High School for, although he was a knowledgeable student of English literature and could quote the masters, he despised his people and his own black self. His clipped English and aristocratic tastes for imported cigarettes, fine clothes, fast women and cars made him a dangerously intriguing personality.

Jacob, who had hoped Frailty might respect the intent of their weekly meeting to gather for fellowship, was irritated to see Frailty go into his briefcase and hurriedly shuffle through a stack of documents. Frailty, one of the ambitious "new breed" Negroes who had become nominally Republican in protest of the traditional Democratic hegemony in southern politics, easily found alliances with whites like Nicholson because they recognized that his position placed him apart from most of his people.

"I can smell Jeanne's cooking," Strop said to prevent Frailty from boring them with a serious discussion.

"Where are our wives?" Grace said.

"In the parlor," thin, leather-skinned Augustus Strop said. He was a man trained at Southern colleges to teach Southern students, a few of whom would go to college to learn to teach.

"Jacob," said Frailty as he boldly laid stacks of papers on the table. "I'm obliged to talk to you seriously . . . "

"After dinner," Jacob said. "There'll be plenty of time."

Jeanne, dressed in a short black rayon uniform that rode up to her knees, trucked bowls of vegetables from the kitchen to the crowded table as the men entered the dining room from the foyer. Grace sat down solemnly and prepared to bless the food. "How do, Jeanne?" he asked the woman absentmindedly.

"Fairly well, Rev'n," Jeanne whispered with liquid voice and proper reverence as she added a cut-glass bowl full of pickles to the table.

Mrs. Strop, chirping like a chick from thin lips that barely moved, stomped into the dining room, walking hard on her heels. At her side, Leah breathlessly waddled from the parlor. Gertrude Grace walked to the door of the living room and leaned on Jacob's arm as they entered the dining room. "How's your dear mother?" she asked. "Ah admire her terrible much."

"She's fine," he said. "I suppose any *old* woman in Mississippi must be respected as a survivor at least."

"What held you up? Nothing serious I hope?" Gertrude asked.

"I was out at Tent City. People who've been evicted from their land are living under horrible conditions."

"How awful. I didn't know such things still existed." A look of incredulity and shock spread over Jacob's face.

Leah, who heard the conversation, tried to save Jacob's face. "If one is in the right place at the right time and knows the right people, one gets ahead. Those people have only their own laziness to blame. These are new times. Times of opportunity," she said.

"Leah's always trying to save me from myself," Jacob correctly observed.

"Exactly," Frailty said. He punched the napkin under his collar, making him look like a pudgy child in a highchair.

"No hiding the truth," Strop conjectured.

Jeanne stared vaguely at the group as they settled down at the table. Mrs. Strop closed her eyes with her chin pointing proudly forward, her back straight as a board. If she washed the powder from her smooth tan skin she might make a handsome woman. The gray of her pressed and oiled hair was a touch of dignity unsuccessfully resisted with dyes. The simple beauty of her body was distorted on every hand by the convention of girdle and unneeded bra. Frailty hung his jowled face on his chest; Augustus Strop, who sat across from his wife, stared in front of himself seeing nothing. Gertrude Grace looked at her husband and then bowed her head and Leah stared at the linen napkin in her lap. Jacob watched all of these people. They all searched for peace and love but were incapable of loving or being loved. A good, confused, utterly harmless people.

Jacob only heard a few words of the preacher's blessing, "Father . . . bless us . . . aid us in . . . " Passing before his mind were a hundred preachers he'd seen over a hundred tables weighted with food and he dreamed of a preacher rousing a people to a feverish pitch while deacons furtively stole through the crowd taking watches, gold, teeth, money and rings from the people who turned into sheep and were led by happy black shepherds to the ovens.

"Oh heavenly Father, please bless those of us who's gathered here in your presence and aid us in struggle and tribulation and aid our businessmen who always give to your church and bless our teachers and doctors who heal our minds and bodies and bless their wives and help us to endure and be patient in these impatient times, for we would now cast off our bonds as in the days of old when Jacob rose up and set his sons and wives upon camels and carried all the cattle and goods that he had got from Laban and stole the images that were his father-in-law's, but give us the wisdom and patience of Laban who forgave . . . In the name of the Father, Son and Holy Ghost, who wear the rainbow for a cape, who wear the stars in their crown, who bow their heads and the heavens weep, I say, amen."

"*Amen*," the diners chanted.

"Preachers always trying to get into a man's pocket," snapped the bulldog face in the blue pin-striped suit.

"Frailty's being barbaric," said Strop from the other end of the table. "Reverting."

"He's not only being crude, he's taking the Lord's name in vain and has proved that athiests have no humanity whatsoever," said Grace.

As Grace piled whipped potatoes onto his plate, he told Mrs. Strop, seated demurely beside him, "I love your perfume, what is it? Such a heavenly flower smell."

"I prefer the earthy smell of a barnyard full of manure," Jacob said, laughing.

"Oh," Mrs. Gertrude Grace cried with pursed lips.

"Here, here," echoed Frailty. "Down with the flowery smell of heaven and funerals and woman."

"That's not proper dinner conversation, Jacob," Leah said.

"You people will have to bear with me," Frailty said. "There are three spoons and four forks at my place. If they're not all gone when I get up, don't be surprised."

Jacob was in another world. It was as though the others at the table spoke a vaguely familiar language. If only they would say something he could hear. Leah, chomping on a piece of chicken, was saying something about carnival . . . Indians only thing interesting to happen . . . this year. Damn Leah and her Creole Association, Women's Auxiliary, Bridge Club and a million daily pastimes.

"Jacob . . . Jacob . . . Jacob . . ." Strop called through the frenzied chatter. "What good do you see coming from this political race you've gotten into?"

The desperate conversations around the table stopped and all turned to hear Jacob's hopefully witty response.

"Good for whom?" he asked.

"For us all," Strop said.

"We'll have a voice in Congress that can speak for better roads, schools, sewers, more jobs and industry and better housing and against inflation and high interest."

"We know all of this," Frailty said. "Why are you running?"

"I believe I'll benefit from any improvement made for the community . . ."

"I want to know one thing, Jacob."

"Go ahead," Jacob urged.

"Do you believe all you tell people? I don't believe you do."

"Of course. Why I've served this community for ten years and I don't think my concern can be questioned." Although he had calculated the potential for viciousness of his friends, he hadn't realized how far it went.

"Well now, isn't this something. Here's a man who's a leading politician finding it necessary to justify himself to us . . ."

So, Jacob thought. That was the trap. In politics there was no such thing as candor. One must distrust those closest to him. He would learn or perish. There was no distinction between his public life and private life.

"I tell you," Frailty said. "The only hope for the race, the hope for the nation, is to develop a strong two-party system."

"You and Rockefeller," Jacob said.

Jeanne disappeared through the swinging kitchen door as Grace whispered, "Terrible Christians. She's a naughty, naughty girl and her mother's notorious."

Grace, plodding day to day from vesper group to bible club to mason lodge, plodding through sticky arguments. Jacob exploded, "Show me one good Christian in this town."

"You come to church an' ah'll show you good Christians," Grace exclaimed.

The telephone's chimes sounded as Jacob continued, attracting the hostile stares of the diners, "I've never met a man who was what he said a Christian should be."

"Ah, the philosopher again," laughed Leah.

"We got our own Faust . . . our own Don Quixote," Strop said ingenuously. "Although I believe in a personal God and that the Lord died to wash away my sins, I also believe in what Jacob said. I became Episcopal to get away from the darkness of the Baptist church—pardon me Reverend—with its ranting and frothing at the mouth."

"Have you ever heard of Bahai?" Mrs. Strop said.

"What kind of game's that?" Frailty said.

"It's a new religion. It believes the new Messiah has come in modern times."

"We're studying it," Strop said.

"Phone," Jeanne called from the kitchen door.

"Take a message."

"It's the Sheriff."

Jacob excused himself and walked into the kitchen.

"The Sheriff probably has a stomach ache," Jacob heard Leah say.

In the kitchen, the voices of the diners were distant murmurs and the Sheriff's slow high cracked drawl was full of immediacy. "Hello, Doc. How's the wife?"

As Jacob listened to the Sheriff he watched Jeanne sitting on a kitchen stool reading the *Courier*. She read it as one must usually read a Negro newspaper, with a glass, occasionally turning it upside down to read misplaced type or furiously searching through the paper for a nonexistant continuation.

"Are you there? Jacob . . ."

"Wife's fairly well, sir. What can I do for you, Sheriff Tate?"

"Sorry ta take ya from your dinner, Doc, but we need ya down here at da jail," the Sheriff said with his voice full of satanic, ironic humor.

"An emergency?" Jacob pleaded.

Jeanne was admiring the pictures on the social page, flipping the pages from one to the other and back again.

"Caught one of them Communist agitators, Doc. He put up a fight an' we had to use persuasion to convince the bastard he should be arrested."

Frightened, Jacob asked, "What's that got to do with me?" Another way to ruin him, he thought.

"We asked every other doctor in town. They're all busy. You comin'?"

Jacob stared at the phone and his hand that held it and let them both fall. He looked up into Jeanne's questioning eyes.

"Fellow sick at the jail," he said. He pulled off his smoking jacket, put on his coat, and snatched up his satchel as he ran to the doorway of the dining room.

"Emergency," he announced. "I hate to leave you folks but . . ."

"Don't be away too damn long, man, or you'll miss the card game," Strop said. "I'm going to make a killing tonight."

"I won't be here when you return," Frailty said, walking Jacob to the door. "I have another engagement. But I must talk to you. There are some papers. When will you be free?" he said despairingly.

"I'll call you," Jacob lied.

"How about lunch tomorrow at the Key Club?"

"Oh, it's integrated now?"

"For several weeks," Frailty said. "Things are changing."

"I'll call."

Leah got up from the table and joined Jacob at the door. "What is it?"

"A prisoner the other doctors won't treat."

"It's not a trick, is it?"

"It'll be all right."

Working through the noisy Thursday streets, Jacob found a usually scarce parking place for his '60 Ford in the municipal lot. He then crossed the square to the courthouse with a lazy long loping step carrying his large body quickly along. A spotlight outlined the statue of a Matchez Indian topping the courthouse peacefully surveying the melee below of shoppers and fun-lovers whose day had not yet really begun, business-minded people, loafers and drugstore philosophers. They lazily buzzed through the dusty streets, honking horns, greeting friends and, in the spirit of democracy, minding everybody's business.

Jacob briskly passed the young country crowd in blue jeans and boots that gathered weekly at the statue of G. H. Woodhouser, local Confederate Civil War hero. The boys' lovely cupid faces with their cow licks and freckles were dumb with an inbred hate for the black man walking among them. They spat automatically on the sidewalk where he passed. He climbed the seventy steps to the white columned courthouse and walked into the cool of the building. Above the portal were the words "EQUAL JUSTICE TO ALL NO MATTER WHAT HIS STATION OR PERSUASION IN LIFE." A few old white farmers slouching around the columns watched Jacob out of the corners of their eyes. The dried old men looked sad but had been that way since birth. "Damned-to-hell nigger commy," one sweetly smelling dried country man said. "Love ta kill that black shit . . ." another man said with a lazy conversational drawl.

The thought that the call may have been a plan to set him up and that all of his plans for the future might end right there in the jailhouse brought time to a halt for Jacob. In the Sheriff's office, sprawled across a chair and a desk, somehow, Bernard Nicholson with a nickel-plated .38 strapped conspicuously to his side scratched his prick while an obese red-faced deputy picked out letters to punch at a typewriter stuffed with some long form. "Damn this fucking typewriter," growled the deputy.

"It don't spell, do it," Bernard said.

Jacob fought to keep the least falter from his voice or movement, but as he began to sense that the men were ignoring him and playing with him it became an inhuman effort to act with a semblance of calm. Or was it his imagination? Perhaps they were just busy and preoccupied. More devastating than certainty, doubt of the intentions of the others in the room gnawed at his mind.

Jacob felt relieved as he became certain of the game and his anger mounted. While the Sheriff read a newspaper at a desk separated from the rest of the office by a low wood partition, the deputy and Bernard looked at Jacob with a slightly amused air and allowed him to stand silently at the counter until the Sheriff, pretending to sense his presence, put the paper down.

"Hello, Jacob. Didn't waste no time gettin' here," the butch-hair-cut Sheriff said. Tate, who had a fatherly streak of gray in his hair, slowly smoked a pipe and had about him the cold air that always surrounds violent men.

Jacob moved to the edge of the Sheriff's desk, sorry that he'd believed him on the phone. Why did Tate and Bernard really want him? "Always willin' to help," he said. He searched their eyes for some sign of respect or compassion.

"How's your maw?" Bernard Nicholson asked. The concern that men like Nicholson had for all the black men and women who'd ever been on their plantations sickened Jacob. "Fine," Jacob said.

"Mighty happy you come, Jacob. Couldn't get none o' these other sawbones," Tate said. "Don't want this prisoner to die. Seems his appendix might o' bust."

"Why didn't you send him to the hospital?" Jacob asked, at once realizing how ridiculous his question sounded.

"We want you to look at him first," the Sheriff smiled.

The six-foot-tall two-hundred-and-fifty-pound deputy at the typewriter girlishly giggled. The evening was hot and a black fan hanging from the ceiling like a large black bird lazily flicked its greasy blades. Covering one wall of the room was a fearful rack straining to hold two rows of shotguns and rifles locked with chains through the trigger guards. Large green army lockers with faded signs stood on the floor below the gun racks: "TEAR GAS, DO NOT USE IN CROWDS."

"What should I put down as reason for arrest on dis warrant?" the typer asked.

"Trespassin', armed insurrection, indecent exposure, bigamy

and resisting arrest ought to do it," Bernard said. The slow clack, clack, clack of the type machine took up again.

The gold badge pasted on the light gray uniform was polished to a high sheen. Light glanced from Jacob's eyeglasses making his eyes invisible. "May I see the patient, Sheriff?" Jacob asked.

Jacob turned from Tate and followed the other lawman out of the office through a series of barred doors opened with keys from a large ring on the deputy's side. Hollow crashing sounds, painful to the ear, came from the walls as counterweights shifted to allow doors to open. The red-faced deputy pushed a button at the elevator. A bell rang and an elevator lazily slid to their floor level. They ascended to the top floor of the courthouse in silence in the cramped car padded with soiled matting spattered full of blood and they kept going until a pudgy white nose jumped into the window of the elevator and red eyes squinted at them and they heard the metallic sound of heavy keys turning the lock of the elevator door which opened to a room lined with reinforced steel doors. The turnkey opened one of the doors and asked Jacob to step into a steel cubical behind it. Jacob warily entered the room. How many had come this way only to leave insane or dead? The door slammed closed behind him. He was alone in a small blazingly lit cubical. The light was blinding sharp and cutting. A small slit opened in the door he had passed and in the slit the turnkey's red eyes beamed. Heavy weights rolled and fell in the wall. They were the bowling-alley sounds that he'd heard downstairs as doors opened. Inside the ceiling there was pounding. For many this had proved to be the very bowels of hell. Jacob doubted that he'd be able to leave. "Push the door in front o' ya an' walk straight ahead," the red eyes said. His stomach tightened and rumbled with an abundance of food. He felt sick.

He obediently pushed at what appeared to be a wall and it swung out of his path. In front of him was a wall of doors. He thought that someone had played a horrible trick on him. He stood facing about ten locked and bolted reinforced doors of the kind one might find in a submarine or ship. One of the doors automatically rolled aside and beyond he could see a row of cells. In one of the cells, curled in the corner, was a black man with the instinctively alert look of an injured animal. Then he realized it was Jesse there in that icy boxlike cubical.

"Do you love me?" screamed an inhumanly pugnacious voice somewhere outside the cellblock. Probably a prisoner in another cellblock. "Oh yes," shouted a high-pitched voice from a closer point in the building. Jesse's eyes, grown large as a doe's and reddened, lowered as Jacob entered the steel closet. The corner of his lips twitched, calling Jacob's attention to a drop of dried blood suspended near his mouth.

He couldn't take Jesse in his arms and walk out with him. The fact overwhelmed Jacob and he thought he might start dry swallowing. He fought the urge.

"I don't need no help, Doc," Jesse said. "I know what I got to do." He punched one fist into the other. His total physiognomy had been revolutionized in the few hours since they'd parted.

"Great God. What have they done to you?" Jacob said, moving to his side and opening his bag.

"They caught me leaving Tent City. They were watching all the roads."

Jacob looked into Jesse's eyes and they both understood that he'd been spared and why. The violence was always selective.

"How much you love meeeeee?" the voice deep within the steel and concrete building plaintively cooed.

"They want to kill me," Jesse said. The cell smelled of urine. There were four steel walls, a steel ceiling and cement floor. The shit-stained hole in the floor overflowed with feces. Jacob touched Jesse's wrists and as the arm was jerked back he noticed welts and bruises.

"Wrist breakers." Jesse extended his arms revealing burns,

"Electric shocks," he calmly explained. Pointing to his genital organ he clenched his teeth and grunted, "They used it there too."

Jacob gave Jesse a shot and some salve. "Put this on your burns. Your cuts too." Jacob's body tensed as he heard the weights roll in the wall. Jesse pressed his back against the wet wall.

Condensation had moistened the steel bars. The smell of the hole filled the room. A yellow 250-watt bulb swung on a cord in the hall making an eternal day. Defiant rivets on the walls and ceiling in ranks and rows formed a strange pattern.

"I don't know how it'll be," Jesse said. "Maybe a prisoner will slit my throat, maybe the beast will shoot me and say I tried to escape, maybe they'll just dump me in the river. I don't know, but it will come. For no reason."

A fat black-garbed minister of God with a conspicuously white collar tiptoed past the cell. "You see the MF that just snuck past? He's goin' to speak to a condemned man. You see the door at the other end of the hall? That's where the state officially lynches."

Jacob was all at once embarrassed, as he was always embarrassed to hear another man's fear. "Listen, don't worry. We'll get you right out." Both Jacob and Jesse understood the nature of the scene Jesse was making: ministers, petty saviors who save no one, stupid religious men coming to the cells asking if you're Protestant, Catholic or Jew as though they're selling cigarettes, talking about grace and salvation, which makes no difference to prisoners who in any case are still imprisoned, who solve problems read in books about salvation and contrition which can only be solved for the ministers themselves. And the life centering around meals, grits in the morning, shit on a shingle for lunch, food tasting like the cell smells, biscuits and molasses for dinner.

"Do you know what's going to happen if we win?"

"What?" Jacob asked.

"Nothing. And do you know what'll happen in this state if we lose?"

Jacob raised one of his eyebrows in a questioning manner.

"Nothing," Jesse said. "On your way out do me a favor? The light. Turn the light out." He held his hand before his face as though to block the light from injuring his eyes.

At first Jacob thought, damn, he might as well have asked for the moon. But then he saw a way. He walked to the spot below the light and reached on tiptoe. He burned his finger and reached into his back pocket for a handkerchief, stretched on his toes and unscrewed the bulb. Fear nibbled at Jacob's back as he ran down the hall and called to be let out. In the dark he called again, louder, "Let me out."

His fear didn't leave him until he descended the elevator in its stifling embrace and rushed from the building to the cool air of the dark Mississippi night. From the darkening sky, the swamp, the shadows of the courthouse, the hundreds of shot, lynched, mangled, consumptive, worn-out, deceased, pickled bodies he'd examined and written "heart attack" on the death certificate screamed at his back. He looked around. No one was there. He took out his handkerchief, turned it over to make sure he didn't get any dirt on his face from the lightbulb, and wiped his brow.

The Southern Arms Restaurant across the square was brilliantly lit with a crowd milling in front—fresh thin white girls eating hot dogs, blue-jean-clad boys, stale looking fat red-faced old men and baggy women who chewed and spat on the walk. A certain part of Southern society was socializing. Jacob jumped in his car and raced down Magnolia Street toward Electric Avenue. Only after he crossed the tracks on Electric near Frailty's Funeral Home did he slow down.

7

Bernard Nicholson and the Other Good Citizens and Leading Families of Matchez

"JACOB," BERNARD CALLED after the tall, well dressed Negro running down the courthouse steps. "Jacob, your wife's on the phone." Jacob, not hearing, kept on going.

As Bernard returned to the Sheriff's office his hand slid up his leg to fondle his gun. Carrying a pistol was, at times, like having a festering sore at his side. At times the weight of the weapon would seem to unbalance his body almost causing him to fall. It caused an ungentlemanly swagger. And many times the gun was something to fondle with a finger, something you wanted to lick with your tongue. To fire the barking machine was wonderous magic. For as quickly as you willed it a hole appeared in the target, or a man was thrown from his feet never to rise again. It was strange how guns in other people's hands looked like toys but when in your own calm hand they became a burden bound by laws, religious dictates and superstitions.

"Couldn't catch him, huh?" Tate asked, looking up from a pile of papers on his desk.

"No."

Tate picked up a phone that lay on his desk and pressed a flashing button. "Sorry, Mrs. Blue, but he just left . . . yes mam," he said and hung up.

"Looks like he's runnin' scared to me," said the deputy.

"He's got reason," Tate said.

"What you mean?" Bernard asked.

"I hear the Klan's gettin' ready. Don't rightly know, though. Just something I heard," Tate said.

"Ain't no more Klan," Bernard said. "Thing ain't done that way no more."

The deputy looked up from his typewriter like a cat who wondered whether he would be drowned.

"Jacob's got every right to run as any other of our respectable colored folks or white folks. It's them outside agitators like the one upstairs we got to watch."

"Sure been a hard day," Tate said, placing his left hand on his right shoulder and stretching his arm.

"Soon as that trustee comes in we can close up," the deputy said.

"You don't think he's flyin', do you?"

"Hell no. He gets out tomorrow. Besides, where'd a mean ugly black like Puddin' hide? Bet his old lady wouldn't even hide him."

Tate beamed good-naturedly and chuckled contentedly as he

cleared up his desk. On his desk was a picture of himself with a couple of hunting dogs, a typewriter, a baseball calendar, a grotesque clay ash tray made by his kids out of Mississippi clay dug in his back yard, and a pile of forms he was required to fill out from the state government.

A very muscular and very black man glided into the room. Unsuccessful in his attempt to diminish his form, he walked with soft treads into the wavering light beneath the fan.

" 'Ere's our nigger. We was about to send the dogs after you, boy," Tate said.

"You late, boy," Bernard added. "Weren't thinkin' of runnin', were you?"

Everyone in the room knew the black prisoner standing before Tate and Bernard should have snatched his cap from his freshly barbered gray head and bent raglike at the waist in a bow and said, no suh, boss, this boy weren't thinkin' of runnin', and then they could laugh. But he only stood there staring at them from eyes that had no pupils. He had won, Bernard thought, for he had stood there too long without answering already and a pistol whipping couldn't erase the fact that he'd already stood there too long. How a nigger that mean had grown that old was a mystery to Bernard. "Boy, you so ugly, I don't see how you stand to live. If I was a nigger, I'd curl up and die from shame like a poisoned dog," Bernard said. Tate laughed. The deputy howled with laughter and shooed the prisoner into his cell.

As the shiny new police car sped screaming down the highway with the speedometer bouncing around in the high numbers, Bernard and Tate lowered their windows to catch the breeze. A shotgun cradled in a bracket between the plastic-covered front seats stuck up between driver and passenger.

"Clayton might find Jesse guilty, but it won't stand up in the higher courts."

"That's okay by me," Bernard said. "And when he gets out, we'll find another reason to arrest him, and another."

"Law enforcement ain't what it used to be," Tate said. "Once you didn't need a warrant, you'd just knock a suspect on the head and throw him in jail. The courts would uphold it. But now you need a warrant to git a conviction. The public today seems to protect criminals."

"The influence of the North, the federal government . . . "

"Being sheriff's a complicated business. You not only have to know the law, you have to enforce it. Take liquor. Liquor's illegal to sell in the state, but we got to tax the people who make and sell it."

"Then every election time a liquor joint has to be raided to keep the ministers happy," Bernard said.

"Yep, Sheriff has to be lawyer and politician. Has to have brains enough to know his friends and enemies and be almost smart enough to figure God's plan."

After high school Tate had worked unsuccessfully at his family's cattle business but, failing to keep it going after his father died, had planted trees on the land and used what prestige his family retained to get the job as sheriff. "You cut any pulpwood this year?" Bernard asked.

"I drug me enough logs out of there to pay ma taxes and put a little money in my pocket. Guess I'm through cutting this year. Had to use a jackleg outfit. Otherwise the tax boys want a third of the profit."

They passed St. Puce's Cathedral on Main Street. On top of the church was a tall spire surmounted by an illuminated cross. Bernard caught a glimpse of a picture of Christ inside the church behind the blazing altars of gold and Carrara marble. Many years ago the church had received a bell from Rome. A well-kept cemetery adjoining the church was surrounded by a high fence for fear that someone would steal the head stones or worse. In the middle of the graveyard of seamen, scouts, adventurers, distinguished veterans of the American Revolution, and French, Spanish, English and American notables was a monument to the Confederacy. A gigantic oak in the graveyard was reported to have been a tree under which the Matchez Indians met.

It was these people, Bernard was certain, these Catholics allied with the New York Jews and niggers, who were ruining his father. Why just the other day the Federal Reserve pushed up the discount rate, making it harder for his father's bank to borrow money. But how do you fight Wall Street when they want to channel all money for investment out of savings banks into the war and commercial banks?

Near Pearl Street they could see the alluvial bluffs of Louisiana rising above the Mississippi. Bernard could barely make out the small sandbar on the river where many of the town's leading families had ended arguments with duels. "Those were the days," Bernard said.

"What?"

"When they used to fight it out, out on the sandbar."

"It's against the law," Tate said. "The reconstruction government outlawed dueling. Law's still on the books."

"These elections sure has turned the town upside down," Bernard said.

"What're we goin' to do 'bout that Blue nigger?" Tate asked. "He may win the election what with our folk split up the way they is, Republican and Dixiecrat."

"Machiavelli."

"What? Mack who?"

"Machiavelli. You should read him," Bernard said. "The only philosopher worth following. He points out things like how a ruler should crush enemies who cannot be won, how promises only have to be honored when they're in your favor, how it's better to be feared than loved but easier to rule with kindness. And how a prince shouldn't give people liberty, but only comfort them with the appearance of liberty."

"He from anywhere around these parts?" the Sheriff asked. "I'd like to talk to that fellow. Sounds right smart."

"No, he's dead."

"Who killed him? Hope they hanged 'im."

Bernard laughed at the Sheriff's naïveté and said, "My great-granddaddy went to the Congo and West Indies and bought the great granddaddies of half the niggers we got in this town. I know how to handle them! Don't worry."

The Greek Revivial mansion he called home sent a warm glow throughout Bernard's chest, rising as it did from the fertile ground, the white columned, porticoed and pedimented house he'd been raised in. A few nondescript towers lost themselves among moss-covered tops of trees. From the lighted house opaque obliques of light shone through the fanlight above the door. Bernard jumped from the car and waved to the Sheriff as he turned around and drove back out the drive. Bernard let the heavy knocker fall at the front door and opened it. It was rarely locked.

Near one of the staircases that rose to the right and left of a tall oak door ornately carved, stood Reverend Hosea Gilsby, the radio preacher, talking to Ethel Wisner. Guests were standing on the balcony drinking. A few formally dressed people sat on the teakwood stairs that rose to the balcony. The house had been a playhouse to Bernard in his youth, a buttress against the chaotic Matchez community that roamed the streets. The study, he'd learned from his tutors and his father, was a place where river pirates had met and adventurers once plotted, the main hall was where society stole dishonest glimpses of each other, the bedrooms allowed dishonesty between wife, husband, brother and sister behind locked doors and the kitchen was separated from the main house for fear of the fires that burned there tended by slaves.

Mr. Ephram Lorchman and his wife, Janice, were perspiring as they furiously chatted. Ephram, a fellow whose father had made good in the garment industry and who'd used his family wealth to invest in some large downtown stores, was telling a simple story Bernard had heard him tell a hundred times, but had never listened to carefully, about a woman who embarrassed herself by reaching in her bosom for a handkerchief.

"Bernard, darling," Janice said, seeing him approach. She kissed him wetly on the lips. Ephram hugged him, "Good to see you, Bernie." He smiled and moved on.

Schneider was standing nearby talking to a tall blonde with sardine-colored lipstick that seemed out of place on her thin pink lips. He wore a double-breasted pin-striped suit over a matching vest. "While you were in New England did you chance to meet a hilariously unscrupulous financier who goes under the name of Charles Grady?" Schneider asked. "Yes," the girl responded as Bernard passed. "Say all you want to about Charles, but remember he's basically good at heart."

"Bernard," Colonel Brady said, extending his hand. Colonel Brady, who only came around during fox-hunt season, was his father's favorite hunting partner.

Old Alton and Lucy Tilly were helping themselves to hors d'oeuvres served by a dinner-jacketed waiter when they saw Bernard and rushed toward him with open arms. "Bernie, baby," Lucy said with her husky voice.

"Have you seen Laura?" Bernard asked.

"I think she's on the veranda, darling," Lucy said.

On his way to the veranda he passed John Hansen, a builder and landowner who'd probably just come from the meeting of the insurance commissioners. He sat comfortably in the deep cushions of an armchair.

Mrs. Wisner seemed to be enjoying a light conversation with one of her pupils who was covered with lace and crinoline. "Bernard, I want you to meet Sally Turner Reeves," Mrs. Wisner said. The girl blushed. He bowed quickly and excused himself.

Anastas Zakis, the owner of several prominent restaurants and key clubs, was enjoying an argument with Al Mizel about whether to use a dry fly or a spoon with bass in the swamp.

Art Reid, an insurance man who'd just been appointed to a

minor post with the state insurance commission, was speaking to Elizabeth Fletcher, the wife of General Hal Bleumont, Mississippi National Guard chief, about how to grow mums. Bernard hurried past them and the wife of the president of the University of Mississippi, who was explaining a recipe to someone for an oriental dish she'd tasted on a recent trip to Japan.

In the crowd he neared the Beuforts and their son who were speaking to Mr. Nelson, an old friend of the family.

"It's beastly of you to run a little fox down like that," Terressa McCloud Beufort III was saying.

"What about the wear and tear on the hunter? Have you no pity on us?" Straughton Nelson said.

"How about that, Bernard?" Ralph Beufort III said, seeing Bernard nearby.

Grabbing a drink from a tray held by a waiter, Bernard said, "Remember the dogs last year who ran up on a wild boar and were ripped apart? Let's drink to them."

"How ghastly," Mrs. Beufort said.

Bernard finally found Laura on a bench near the pond with Judge Clayton.

"Bernie," she said, rising to embrace him.

"It's getting cool out here," the Judge noted as they started in toward the house. "I had a whole parcel of things to speak to you about, but maybe we better make it another time," Clayton said. Bernard took one arm and Laura the other as much out of respect as to steady the old fellow.

Bernard found Laura's cotton dress, swept around her like mist from the river, pleasing. He would have to do something to tie this woman down, he thought, or she would do some silly thing like marry a man with no money or dedicate herself to a profession. Perhaps he'd make her pregnant. That would be the smart way to do it. That'd stop all of her preaching about independence.

8

The Impostor

JAMES, WITH THE STOICISM that had seen him safely
through all natures of danger, showed Frailty in. In the hall,
which impressed Frailty with its brilliance and gave him the
feeling that these were, after all, the halls that intelligent and
ambitious persons such as himself were entitled to tresspass,
Frailty saw Schneider, Ethel Wisner, old Sam Nicholson, young
Bernard and Miss Laura Dunn all crowding around Judge
Clayton.

"Unlimited potential. There's no end to the good that can
come . . . " Clayton was saying. Bernard left the group and
walked briskly toward Frailty with outstretched hand. "How are

you, good to see you, have you eaten?" he asked, pointing to the dining hall where a glittering table was loaded with lobsters, crabs, hams, and turkeys. "Yes, sir," Frailty said. "Well come and let's introduce you to the guests." Bernard whispered his name to an attendant at the door who, after the orchestra heralded him, announced his name to the group.

Frailty was completely at ease then. As a matter of fact his whole body was soothed with gross satisfaction. Bernard darted away from Frailty to attend a lady who waved her handkerchief at him and Frailty was launched alone on the social sea of the upper crust of Matchez.

Janice Lorchman, who had been nibbling on an olive, bit down hard on the plastic pick holding the green fruit. Ephram, noting her shock, twisted slightly around raising his eyebrow. Colonel Brady walked quickly toward the door, asking a waiter nearby to get his coat and hat. "Who is that handsome man that just walked in?" Lucy Tilly asked. Alton, making a superhuman effort to control himself, said, "Frailty, I believe they said his name was." Interrupting an embarrassing moment of silence Terressa McCloud Beufort said, "What do you do with the fox when you run it down?"

"We shoot it and cut its ears and tail clean off," Straughton Nelson said.

"Did you see that?" Art Reid said, referring to Colonel Brady's walkout.

"Some people are such boors," said Elizabeth Fletcher, a woman of ambition and strong will who kept her maiden name after marriage. "I'm so tired of people talking about black this and white that. I really don't see any difference in people. People are people, you know, the world over. Why when I was in Brazil I was so happy to get away from such troublesome bickering about race. I do believe if we can just strengthen the United Nations that within our lifetime we'll see the end of all world struggles, what do you think?"

Frailty, who was beginning to feel like flotsam on the social tide, made his way accross the room toward a dark face he caught a glimpse of through the crowd. He wondered if the fellow were from out of town or out of state. He might even be from another country, for Frailty knew that among the rich entertaining African dignitaries was popular. If he were from another country, Frailty hoped his English was good and they'd be able to talk. As he approached, the other fellow started walking toward him. When they met Frailty extended his hand. The fellow dressed in a tuxedo took his hand and pulled him close to whisper in his ear. "Hey man, what room you working tonight?"

"I'm a guest," Frailty said coldly.

"Pardon me," the fellow said haughtily.

Again Frailty was alone, and then slightly bewildered.

Frailty stood in the center of the brilliantly lighted room full of ripples and eddies of conversation chewing on a tiny sandwich and sipping a cocktail he knew would give him indigestion until Bernard and Judge Clayton approached him and led him into a book-lined room with a long walnut table in it. Several other men wandered into the room and took their places at the table each checking the place card to ascertain if he'd found the correct seat. Bernard showed Frailty to a seat that had a card, like the rest, with his name and coat of arms. Frailty was suddenly afraid. On his card was a sphinx with negroid features. Were they going to make fun of him? he wondered. He looked with dismay at his hands, so black in contrast to his white shirt.

"I see you're a son of Egypt?" Clayton said, sitting beside Frailty.

The son-of-a-bitch was sounding on him. What could he do? He should never have come.

"I find the period of Ethiopian rule of Egypt very interesting," the man said.

Say, Frailty thought. The white bastard was serious. Frailty stared into the blue eyes of the white-haired judge.

"When I was in Timbuktu I found documents which mentioned the rule of the Mandingoes. That's an exciting story, don't you agree?"

"Yes," Frailty lied. "I've always found that story exciting. One of my favorites."

Bernard Nicholson rose at the head of the table while raising his arm demanding silence. "We have gathered here for a grave purpose," he said. "A citizen of our town who has helped in its growth is here tonight and before he leaves we must initiate him into the ranks of Southern Gentlemen. But first he must have bestowed upon him the proper uniform of a Southern Gentleman. Therefore, he must understand the proper uniform of a Southern Gentleman."

Frailty looked around the table at the stern face of Lorchman, the deceptively soft face of Schneider, the cold dark eyes of Alton Tilly, Zakis who seemed to be molded in stone after a classical design, an unsmiling military man and some men from the Jackson comptroller's office whose thin boney mountain faces certainly must mask some horrible knowledge, and he shivered.

"Shortly after the Revolutionary War," Bernard said, exaggerating his drawl, "there migrated to the South many bold venturesome men. Many of them were about two jumps ahead of a Virginia sheriff or a Maryland mob." Schneider muffled a snicker. Bernard continued his story with a straight face. "Upon their arrival at Cumberland Gap or whatever point they entered the South they, like butterflies emerging from a cocoon, shed their former drab personalities and emerged in this virgin territory in a newly founded glory of colonels, and majors and admirals. Those of lesser value, as well as those of small ambition, migrated further south where they were known under the title of captain, which is still a popular title in Mississippi,

Tennessee and Alabama. At that time the colonels' characteristic insignia consisted of a brace of dueling pistols, a plug of
chewing tobacco, an overwhelming desire to hunt, fight or make
love to some woman and a quart of bourbon whiskey. Later
when the success and riches of this new land became theirs
generally through luck at cards and not as a result of industry or
work, the regalia of the Southern colonel was a broad-brimmed
hat, a frock coat, a pair of baggy trousers and a shoe-string
necktie. To this he added a white goatee, a pair of sideburns, a
veneer of culture and a quart of bourbon whiskey." Lorchman,
Schneider, Zakis and most of the others were laughing or smiling. "At a later period," Bernard continued, looking a little
devilish now that his trick was out of the bag, "after the unfor-
tunate war, known as the war of the rebellion, war of the
Southern Confederacy or as my grandfather called it, the late
unpleasance among the states . . ." Old man Nicholson gave
a rebel yell at that point almost throwing Frailty from his seat
with its vigor. "Well, then the colonel's uniform consisted of a
pair of patchy gray pants, a floppy-brimmed hat, a tobacco-
stained goatee and a quart of bourbon whiskey, which produced
in him a marked dislike for anything Northern. Around the
turn of the century the colonel's uniform consisted of mutton-
chop whiskers, a broad-brimmed hat, a broad-clothed Prince
Albert suit, love for the Democratic Party and a quart of
bourbon whiskey. In the last days of the decline of Southern
colonels due to the encroachment of Yankee ideas and customs
about the only portion of any uniform left is a quart of bourbon
whiskey."

Everyone raised whiskey glasses and drank, "To the South,"
Lorchman said. "To Southern colonels," Schneider said. "To
Colonel Frailty," Bernard laughed.

"Speech," the General called. "Speech," Sam Clayton demanded, striking the table.

"John Frailty," Bernard said. "As a part of your initiation

into the highly secretive organization known as the Liar's Club whose name is not to leave this room, which is dedicated to tall stories, drinking and good food . . ."

"And good women . . ." Clayton said, nudging Frailty with a devilish grin on his face.

"We would like to hear a few words from you."

Frailty stood. He was sweating, but he refused, out of principle, to use his handkerchief to wipe the beads of perspiration from his brow; an act he'd perform with flourish before a black audience. All his life he'd hustled. This would have to be the best and biggest hustle of his life. He'd always told himself that you can't out fight the Man, because he has all the guns, and you can't buy him out, because he has all the money, but you could always run a line on him. Tell them what they wanted to hear.

"Gentlemen," Frailty said. He should limit the use of histronics, he thought. "My people has . . . er, have been a great people ruling Egypt and Ethiopia and many great African kingdoms. After great strife and suffering a large number of us have come to this land where we have helped build a great nation. Today, though, we ain't a bitter people, but rather, a grateful people for the bounty the land has shown us," he said, getting ready to go into an enlightened conservative speech. Clayton was smiling and nodding his head. He looked to Frailty like a man who should be home where a nurse could change him, feed him and dip him a little snuff.

"Foul . . ." Lorchman said.

"Unfair. He's serious. He's not a liar, Bernard," Zakis said.

Schneider walked out saying, "Disgraceful."

"Boooooo," the General started shouting.

Bewildered and completely exhausted, Frailty slumped into his chair.

"Impostor, impostor," Sam Nicholson said.

"Gentlemen, gentlemen," Bernard beseeched, "let us drink to John Frailty's excellent imitation of the speech of the now extinct species of human known as the colored pork-chop preacher or Negro college president."

The room roared with laughter and everyone raised their glasses. Frailty, however, lay slouched in his chair feeling exactly like putty and cursing the day his god had created white folk.

The General stood and said, "Speaking of bourbon whiskey, I was in church a couple of years ago when the preacher was preaching against the evil of drink. He said, 'And do you good folk know that at this very moment several members of our congregation are up by the spring house drinking bourbon whiskey?' At that moment two men stood up and said, 'The preacher done told us where the whiskey is, men, let's get to it.' " The story ended amid the whoops and yells of the men at the table.

Frailty, who wanted to cry, instead armed himself with a deceptive grin. After a few more rounds of toasting and story-telling Frailty excused himself. While walking to the door with Frailty, Bernard explained, "I hope ya had a good time. Some of the fellows take their joking a little too seriously." Frailty was thoroughly confused and drove home with his eyes blurred with tears of rage. He fell in bed fully clothed to stare restlessly at the ceiling, his heart racing, biting his tongue and cursing white folks as his bewildered wife looked silently on.

9

Squeals and Groans

". . . I REMEMBER WHEN I could stay up all night drinking with the fellows the night before the hunt. But I'm a little too old, Bernard," Clayton said as Bernard helped him up the stairs to a guest room. Suddenly two children in pajamas and bathrobes bumped against them, almost knocking them down. Ella, the maid, rushed after them, catching them halfway down the stairs on the banister. She pulled them off and spanked them up the stairs and back into their room. The door slammed and behind it Bernard and Clayton could hear the children's whining protest over the sound of slaps. "When I was their age,"

Clayton said with melancholy, "only Aunt Willa had the guts to tan my hide. My father didn't seem to care and my mother was afraid to do it."

"Art and Mary are modern parents. Don't believe in spanking children. Fortunately they ain't had time to convince Ella of their philosophy. When I was little Ella never wasted words with me either," Bernard said.

Standing at the door of the room where he'd spend the night Clayton said, "Had a lot to talk to you about. Thoughts all muddled now. Be sure and wake me for breakfast. Even though I can't ride with you, nothing quite as appetizing as breakfast on the lawn with hunters."

After saying good night to the Judge, Bernard hunted through the bedrooms and halls for Laura. In one room he heard the squeals and groans of a man hard at some woman. He was about to break into the room on the chance that Laura was therein ensconced when James came down the hall and told him he'd seen Laura leave with Mr. Schneider. Bernard went downstairs to the study where he and other men talked politics, told lies and drank until the sun came up.

10

Goin' On Home

JACOB DROVE OUT Magnolia Street and turned onto Electric Avenue where the tobacco and cotton warehouses formed large hulking night images. He crossed the railroad track slowly so as not to ruin his car and continued on past Frailty's Funeral Home and finally headed up the drive to his house blazing with light. Cars were parked on Mangrum and Electric on the grassy shoulder of the road and a couple of guests had pulled up into the Smith's and Robinson's front yards.

Jacob opened his front door and was struck with the jumping sound of party music and the spectacle of twenty people shouting, dancing and playing. "Congressman Blue," Strop shouted. "Jacob," came shouts from all sides. Leah let go the grip she had on Mrs. Strop's arm and ran to Jacob. "You're just in time. This is sort of a pre-election victory party," she said, pulling Jacob by the coatsleeve. "I was so worried," she said, hugging him. In the brightly lit room punch bowls and trays of nuts, figs, dishes of ham and boned, stuffed duck were scattered about. The night and the liquor had softened everyone's faces so that even Augustus Strop and his wife seemed human and down-to-earth.

Of the three couples that were dancing—most of the dancers were young teachers and danced a carefully stylized version of the latest dance which was, despite its dilution, powerful, but devoid of its necessary sexuality—the most interesting couple was Mrs. Grace and a young fellow who worked for the federal government. Reverend Grace seemed just as amused as the others that the preacher's wife would try out the latest dance steps. Her head, shoulder and arm movements along with the loud hand claps were a mixture of a righteous church sister and a teeny-bopper.

"Leah, pour your husband a drink before he dies of thirst," Strop said. His face gleamed slightly with perspiration. "Everyone's afraid to talk about it," he said, moving close to Jacob's side, "but after all the trouble about the need for a Negro school-board member it seems a waste for them to have appointed Old Man Frailty. What does a funeral director know about education?"

"He was safe," Jacob said. "I don't mind the choice as much as I do the method of choosing," Jacob said. "Bankers and lawyers on the school board shouldn't have the sole authority to choose who'll sit on the board."

"Don't ever tell a soul I told you," Strop said. "But actually they chose Old Man Frailty because they knew if they waited any longer the people in the town would come up with a strong favorite. So they financed his election."

"Unfortunately there's been no opposition," Jacob said.

"People are afraid. Afraid for their jobs. Afraid they'll be called oddballs," Strop whispered. "Teaching is an unholy business. Don't ever tell anyone, but if I could have gotten into a plumber's union, at one point, I would have become a top-notch plumber. But there are so many advantages to teaching. Not only the salary, but the prestige you have with the banks and loan companies. Everything's so neatly arranged, I simply sign my paycheck over to the bank and they take out for savings bonds, mutual stocks, the house note, furniture note, insurance, car note. My wife pays for our groceries. I'd hate to think what'd happen if I were ever ill for a couple of weeks."

Leah handed Jacob an effervescent pink drink. Jacob moved through the crowd toward Grace, who kept one eye on his wife while speaking to Sam Jones, a college graduate who read a lot of books and landed a soft job in the post office after it integrated. He was famous in Jacob's eyes for not complaining. When bricks had started to fall from the post office wall, he'd mentioned it to Jacob and his friends who told him to talk to the boss. After a long talk with his boss he took the initiative to put up a sign reading, "Watch for falling bricks." Once Jacob visited his apartment to call on his invalid grandmother. He remembered one striking physical fact about the house; something in the bathroom of the tenement leaked from the sagging concavity of the ceiling into the wash basin. Although the commode from the apartment above would soon fall into his bathroom, Sam was content that it dripped into his sink and not on the floor. Sam wore a black mohair suit and tapered Italian shoes. He was known to drive the wildest car in town, which he'd come to own because a soft-hearted salesman had broken the installment agreement with Sam by not demanding total payment when Sam missed a month. Now Sam refused to pay the man and by law, the car dealer couldn't repossess the car. He'd have a hard time doing that anyway since Sam hid the car every evening in a friend's back yard. All the women liked Sam and he'd come to Jacob more than once with unwholesome remembrances of females he'd visited. Once he'd let it go so bad he could barely urinate. Poor fellow.

"You haven't seen a thing until you've shopped in the New York garment district," he was telling Reverend Grace. "When I was last there a friend took me down where they make suits and I had a couple tailored for me right in the shop. The suits are better than anything you can buy around here. Why I bought a wash and wear suit last summer downtown that I wore once and washed and it fell apart."

"I know what you mean," Grace said. "I bought my wife four pairs of stockings the other day and she used up a pair a day. They ran or just disintegrated when she tried to wash them. We do most of our shopping for clothes in Jackson or Memphis."

"Jacob," Sam said. "I've been wanting to talk with you about a problem we're having in the post office. The women are taking it over. The segregation for men is as bad as ever, but ever since the '64 civil rights bill gave women the same chance at government jobs as men, they've been taking over the best positions."

"Is it because women are better prepared?" Jacob asked.

"You might say that," Sam said. "But still they shouldn't be allowed jobs men could have." Sam reached out and grabbed Mrs. Strop as she was passing and began dancing with her. At first she was stiff, but she quickly forgot her inhibitions and fell into the easy rhythm.

Augustus Strop watched his wife with his usual obscene stare. The primary problem Strop presented those who would meet him or talk to him was his physiognomy; the aristocratically raised eyebrow and simultaneously lowered eyelid, the arrogant lip that turned up at the corner and the cocked head. "I can remember when you had to ask a man to dance with your wife or escort," he said.

"People don't waste any time these days," Jacob said.

As her body warmed Mrs. Strop was unable to hide her womanly odor in spite of all the usual unguents and so the room gradually filled with the smell of woman, pungent and exciting.

"Jacob. Let me say one thing seriously to you this evening. I doubt if I could say it another time. Take my advice, Jacob. Stay away from those madmen."

"What men?"

"Greeks bearing gifts."

Jacob hated Strop's obsequious bending to unseen powers. "Greeks bearing gifts" had been the warning Strop had spread when Harvard-educated Ed Banks had come to town to teach. Any outsiders were Greeks bearing gifts. Strop had conducted a clever campaign of vilification designed to drive the talented, Mississippi-born Banks from town. In the end, Strop, who had seniority and a close relationship with white educators, simply told Banks there was not enough room in town for both of them. Banks, correctly reasoning that he could get a job in any school system, left Matchez rather than put up an unseemly fight. A white teacher, whose name Jacob couldn't remember, had also been run out by Strop, who'd made race an issue. This time Strop's comment about Greeks bearing gifts evidently referred to the movement. While Jacob would have preferred not to have worked with the strange-looking, weird-acting movement people, they were the only ones who worked for him during his campaign and were the only ones with useful ideas about campaign strategy.

"Strop," Jacob said. "When are you going to stand up and say, NO, I'm not a nigger, I'm a man? Even in the mirror?"

Strop grabbed his wife, Allemenia, by her thin arm and wrenched her to his side. "Darling," he said. "There's a disease running rampant these days. We must all avoid it. It's called martyrdom and it affects the brain." A circle of people formed around Jacob, Allemenia, Strop and Sam Jones, who hoped he could finish the dance. With propitious irony in his voice Strop said, "It would be tragic if Jacob caught the disease for doctors are their own worst patients."

"Your wisdom overwhelms me," Jacob said and made his way to the door. Leah intercepted him at the stairwell and whined, "You can't leave me."

"I'm tired. And I have a phone call to make."

"The only time I see you now is when you come sneaking home to change clothes."

Jacob often wondered what life would have been like with a woman who held the same things dear as he. Although their lives were going in two different directions when they met, he had been attracted to her precisely because of their disparate souls. In one sense she was his other self, reaching for, demanding and possessing all those things he had guilt about owning. She had constantly accused him of complacency about his life's position and pushed him to acquire the house, cars, money and prestige she thought they were entitled to. He looked at her rouge, powdered cheeks, lotion-salved skin and wig masking her for the party and thought it remarkable how close he could be to Leah physically and yet find her true self impregnable. Leah placed her hand inside his jacket and rested it on a secretly sensitive spot at his waist. Her hot breath struck his face. "You've had quite a bit?" he said.

"Suppose I have. I have good goddamn reason to drink. You've insulted our friend Augustus."

"He insults my sensibilities."

"Damn your sensibilities . . ." she said sweetly as a belladonna.

Jacob knew too of Leah's loneliness. He knew that often her breasts swelled and her stomach became upset creating in her, each time it happened, the hope that she might be pregnant. "Poor Strop," Jacob said. "To be a school teacher one must either be a social reformer, a cynic or a drunkard. That's a fact. But Strop has never chosen which sort of creature he should be. So he gives his hand at each in turn."

Leah laughed.

"I have to make a phone call. Be back in a moment."

"If you leave me before we end this evening I'll hate you."

"I'll be back," he said and went into the kitchen. Some strangers were standing around leaning on the refrigerator and counter talking politics. Since he couldn't have heard himself speak in the kitchen he made his call from the study.

Jacob called Brad Wilson and asked him to go next door and get Rachel. When she came to the phone he heard she already knew about the arrest. "A lawyer from Jackson's coming down to try and get Jesse out," she said, "but we can't afford to raise no more bond money. If there's a big bond, he'll just have to stick it out."

"But he thinks they may kill him," Jacob said.

"He has a vivid imagination. He knew what he was getting into before he got in there, anyway."

"It's that cold."

"That cold."

"See you tomorrow about the plans for election day."

"Make it around lunch time," Rachel said. "And don't talk so much on the phone . . . People are listening . . ."

Jacob hung up on the phone and went back into the party where he found Mr. and Mrs. Strop, Grace and his wife seated around a card table. Strop jubilantly slammed his hand of cards down on the table, knocking over a drink. Gertrude Grace screamed. Strop had gin-rummied. "Do you want to sit in?" Grace asked.

Jacob stayed at the card table until early morning. After seeing everyone to the door, Leah went upstairs and fell out on the bed in her clothes. But Jacob roamed about their room, picking up books and putting them down and touching everything in the room as though it were strange to him. Before the sun was up and as the land lightened for the morning, Jacob undressed himself and then tugged Leah's clothes off and climbed in between the cold white sheets.

II

11

Friday, the Morning After

LEAH, WAITING IN HER FRONT HALL for a cab, checked her
watch. She had to be at the church by ten. From where she sat
she could see Jeanne working to clean the front room turned
upside down by the party-makers. As she tied a somber lace
kerchief on her head she thought that she'd simply have to remember to get some extra help to come in and remove the slip
covers from the furniture for the winter. Finally a car honked in
the street.

'The Cathedral, driver,' she told the unbecoming, rough-
looking man behind the wheel.

"You mean the one down on Magnolia?"

"The one and only cathedral, on Magnolia and Main," she said, settling back in the leather seat of the air-conditioned cab.

At St. Puce's she acted outraged to find that the driver would charge her two dollars, but after paying him she asked him to wait for she would have been frightened to be in that section of town without transportation. Straightening her kerchief, she entered the church and found it empty except for one other supplicant and the white-arrayed priest. The praying hands and upturned eyes of the plaster-cast saints, the vertical sweep of the exposed wooden joists drew Leah's eyes to the ceiling where her gaze met an image of a golden-haired man embracing the globe.

She genuflected and joined the other supplicant on her knees before the altar of God. "Holy Mary, Mother of God, blessed is the fruit of thy womb, Jesus, Amen. Holy Mary, Mother of God, pray for us sinners, now and the hour of our death. Blessed . . ."

"God," Leah said in prayer. "Make me pregnant. Give me children or I die. Jacob asks if he is God and is to blame because I'm barren. Oh God," Leah cried. She lay her head upon her arm and sobbed. "My husband has a child by another woman in the city. I don't blame him for loving them, but let me have children that he may love me . . ." Leah didn't bother to follow the Latin words of the priest in the book of translations but was filled with the rhythm of the ancient words. The spondaic pathos of the remorseful words weighed upon her. On the altar a gold cross seemed to burn with a holy brilliancy. Candles shown like stars amid the white and red velvet and silk drapes about the altar. The fat white priest moved with powder-smoothness through the ritual, crossing himself, bowing, lighting candles, turning the pages of a book. Leah cried out softly when the thick soft white hands came near her mouth to place the bread wafer on her lips—the flesh of Christ. And then the blood was drunk and it had the sharp taste of grape wine and made her dizzy to smell it in her mouth. If she only could embrace the corpulent body before her and take it into her mouth like the wine and bread. She shed pious tears.

"Oh Lord, don't let me be pregnant . . ." prayed Laura in the front of the Cathedral on her knees near the yellow-skinned Negro woman. Her red hair was covered by a dark kerchief folded to hide the bright design. "Make me strong enough to stand with Bernard and give to him and walk with him in this hellish world to be his right hand. Help me to give myself only to him." Feeling faint she left the Cathedral to be revived by the outside air. She noticed a colored cabby waiting nearby, no doubt for the other person in the church. Laura looked over the well-kept grounds and thought that the Catholics had such a wonderful sense of order for everything. It was the only civilized way to live—with order and purpose. A baby now, by someone other than Bernard, would spoil her purpose.

12

Rachel

"When the doctor coming?" asked the lady with the snake in her stomach who'd come all the way from Louisiana to see Jacob.

"Soon, soon, just wait dear," her pregnant companion entreated.

"Why doesn't he open the clinic?" a bent and wracked man from Tennessee said.

"I ain't God, honey," the pregnant woman said. "How can I tell you? Just wait like the rest of us."

Dogs barked somewhere in the hills. "That's a bad sign," the lady with the snake said.

"It just white folk hunting a fox," her pregnant friend said. "God save anything that get in their way."

"White folk can think of the strangest tomfoolery."

Jacob sat at his square desk circumscribed by a yellow circle of light from the globe that hung over his head. Jacob's large face floated above his desk, his white shirt only a blur in the bright light. His arm moved in a semicircle turning the leaves of a bible, projecting in space half a cylinder. The thick study curtains closed out the heat and light of day and only a few strands of light passed through the velvet cloth and attached themselves to the floor. He pushed a buzzer on his desk and Mrs. Waters entered from the clinic.

"Reading the bible?" she asked.

"Not just the bible, but a very special bible," Jacob said. "Here's a list of supplies we must order. You're going to have to handle the clinic today. I have to spend a few hours out. If there's an emergency, call me here." He wrote Rachel's number on the note pad.

"Old Lady Bryant is here with another snake in her stomach," Nurse Waters said through a devilish smile.

"Give her another enema and it'll go away."

"Nurse Waters took the list of items and turned to go, hesitated and turned back to say, "I think what you're trying to do is good, but there's some things God didn't mean to change. Least not quick as you might want. Anyway, you're spending too much time away from the clinic. The people need you, Jacob."

"Nurse Waters, I'm out of place in this world. The business of most of us is one of predator. That is why so many people's main ailment is loneliness."

"God help us."

"Don't worry, Nurse. I am not crazy. Even though I pass along a line drawn through the darkest reaches of insanity where lesser lights extinguish themselves. I'll retain my sanity no matter how cruelly they trick us. When we were told the black breasts of our mommas stank—it was a lie—we lived lies. They knew it was a lie for they had tasted that sweet black milk too. Grace, Frailty, Strop, the Nicholsons and Claytons and all the sons of this town prey upon the weak and ignorant and only draw together into a community when the words of a Hitler, a Reverend Gilsby or a Judge Clayton tell us to unite to die. The white clean words coming crisply from the mouths of parents, teachers, friends, enemies and loudspeakers pierce us through cold as steel spears."

"Well, you know what's best for you," Nurse Waters said, placing her hands on her hips and cocking her head, "but you sound like you talkin' trouble t' me . . . trouble," she said, walking from the room.

Jacob ran upstairs and carefully replaced his mother's bible and then, dressed in his London Fog coat, walked in the autumn morning down Electric Avenue toward Magnolia. The sky suddenly darkened. Quick pounding sounds on tin-roofed barns and warehouses startled farmers. Columns of rain piled up to the sky. Jacob walked upon an earth turned into a sheet of water. Fields were pounded to muddy bogs as the land was beaten and flooded with rain. Flooding water cut through deep culverts beside the road and crops were beaten down and crushed. Cotton, wet and heavy, was knocked from the bolls into the mud. High-sided cotton wagons drawn by skinny mules rumbled through the rain toward the gins. Men scampered about covering the cotton with canvas. Jacob passed houses wide open to catch the breeze, revealing one or two rooms stuffed with bedding and wide open back doors and the fields beyond.

Leaves and debris knocked about in the wind and the air itself seemed muddy. The earth and wet air and vague sky congealed into one brown-streaked sheet and Jacob laughed with fear. He shouted to the sky, "Why do you fool and blind us?"

The sudden storm stopped. And sun began to suck water

from the brown bosom of the land. It was muggy and hot. Jacob's old coat was soaked through and clung to his body. Jacob looked at the land and thought of it as waiting for its next trauma as men waited for the next war.

A convict road gang digging up Main Street was in chaos and enjoying it. Workers deep in a pit were up to their knees in liquid red mud. They called, "Coming out boss, coming out boss . . ." The bosses sat in a truck across the street.

"What's wrong?" Jacob asked one of the fellows in a black-and-white striped suit.

"They can't come out the ditch until the cap'in tells 'em. Cap'ins all ran to get out of the rain. You got a cigarette?"

Jacob thought he felt a fever developing and wished he'd gone to the Saunders' or Moore's to get out of the rain. A hundred boy scouts were camped on the northeast steps of the courthouse safely under the portico waiting to be led through the county seat. They would be shown the electric chair and be told that the law kills the unlawful. Those little beasts, Jacob thought, will spy in upon his brothers locked up behind the bare bars of the jail. None of the boy scouts gave any indication that they saw him pass in his ridiculous drenched coat.

A crowd milled around the Southern Arms Restaurant & Hotel enjoying the closeness of one another as cars stopped at the curb to honk their horns and be served shockingly cold drinks at the curbside.

In the section of town called Newtown, on the street called Pearl, Jacob entered the pool hall. The cool fluorescent lights over the green tables emitted a pleasant glow.

"Ain't nothin' in the world more dangerous than a yellow 'oman," Fats was saying. "A yellow 'oman's dangerous as homemade sin." Fats was a "good guy" to most because he knew a lot—he'd been around the world in the army and could talk trash. "How come whites ain't got no ass?" Fats asked as he racked up the globular balls on the precisely shaped and leveled field of cool felt.

"That's shore 'nough right. They the most flat-assed people I ever saw. But that don't bother me much as the fact they ain't got no heart," Bocat said as he chalked his cue stick.

"They got flat asses 'cause they don't never work," J.V. said. "And they ain't got no balls 'cause de women don't like the way they fuck."

"There's conclusive evidence . . ." Fats was saying.

"Don't throw no big words at me motherfuggin' . . ." J.V. lunged as if to smash Fats in the head. Bocat jumped in between them, pretending to separate the mock fighters. "I'm goin' to whip both you. Ain't you got no respect. Doc Blue must think y'all is some real low-life bastards." Bo, Fats, J.V. and the others in the pool hall looked to Jacob.

"I'm surprised to see you here," Jacob said to Bocat. "The Moores are dirt farmers. Your pa is a dirt man. He ain't happy if he can't put somethin' in the ground and see it grow."

"My pa's in jail. I can't do no farmin' in the rain," Bocat said. "They may take me on at the warehouse this afternoon."

"Sho can't. Maybe tomorrow if the sun stay out," J.V. said.

Jacob followed Fats to the back of the pool hall and through a small door into a back room where several men sat at tables nursing brown bottles of beer. "I got the cab drivers all lined up to take people down Monday," Fats said.

"Very efficient," Jacob said. "We'll have to make sure you get some poverty money to fix this place up and make it first class."

"No, Jacob. It ain't like that. I's just doin' what's right. Ya know what the Jew's bible say. If you're not for yourself, who is for ya? Anyway for this place to do the kind of business it does it got to stay the same." Jacob had a beer and left through the front.

Jacob went into Horvitz and Zakis Green Dot Market, full of housewives and school children, to buy food to take with him to the meeting where he was sure to find a hungry horde. Signs around the market advertised pigs' feet, pigs' snouts, pigs' tails, chitterlings, brains, fatbacks and ham and oxtails and specials on turnip greens, mustards and collards, which were selling for an outrageous twenty cents per pound.

"Get out of here you little thieves," Old Man Horvitz yelled. Women looked at him portentously. Jacob saw Dot Moore scoot out the front door with an armful of corn. A couple of other kids with stuffed pockets ran from the market shouting, "He's got a gun." When Jacob saw the white man flick the safety off his revolver and cock it, he called, "Hey, there's no need for that."

"Who the hell are you? Stay out of my way," the store owner shouted. He ran to the door and looked into the empty street. "Who's going to pay for that corn?" he said, walking back to his cash register and putting the revolver back under the cash drawer.

Jacob spoke to the frightened people in the store under the guise of speaking loudly to a lady in a smock and overcoat standing beside him. "That's why folks gotta get together. When farmers can't afford to eat, there's something wrong . . ."

"Okay, buddy, get out o' here," said the nervous little red-faced man from behind a pair of thick glasses. He had one hand on the cash-register drawer.

Jacob, his nerves a jingle, walked from the store. His stomach felt uneasy. He might have been shot.

Jacob passed a ragged-haired man in a gigantic overcoat who begged a quarter and then backed away from him bowing. Sitting on porches covered with green potted plants old men called "how do" to him. Sticking up from little clay and dust yards were porcelain images of ducks, the white Virgin, black bootblacks, black dogs, white Jesus and other assorted colorful characters. Those were the houses of mill, waterfront and factory laborers, who were constantly in search of a home with grass and trees around it but who were limited to houses used by other races who left their mark; a crucifix left on the wall left by an Italian Catholic railroad family, a dusty trunk left by a Swedish logger.

Young girls on the street turned their eyes down shamefully to avoid the red glare of Jacob's eyes. Weary old women warmly smiled from the porches where they rocked and watched children playing in the yard and street. Pretending to fish in the gutter with worms crucified on bobbypins and tied to sticks with twine, children were fascinated by the dirty stream running beside the road.

Tina was down at Lorchman and Nelson's when Jacob passed. He could hear her argument with the clothier from the street. "How come a bolt of cloth cost so much?"

"Prices everywhere goin' up. It's the war, inflation," Lorchman said.

Tina came out the front door of the store and bumped into Dot. Jacob watched the two collide on the sidewalk.

"Ma," Dot shouted breathlessly. "Look at the corn what ah stole."

Tina smacked her across the mouth and the corn flew into the street. "Don't let me ever hear you say you stole." Tina said, bending down to help Dot pick up the food. "You was taking what the Lord know belong to usn."

Each battered door Jacob passed on the damp brown street that smelled of cooking, disinfectant and rotting wood, hummed with music or loud talk.

"Man you can get yo' black ass out o' here you goin' to act like dat."

" 'Oman you best get some sense in yo' haid or do I gotta knock it in?"

And at another door he heard, "Little Sally Waters sittin' in a saucer, rise Sally rise," as the children's voices chanted in unison. "Shake it to the East, shake it to the West, shake it to the one you like the best." They clapped their hands while singing.

Jacob felt drained of energy as he knocked at the dreary door of the Water Street row house. The house, one of those peculiar houses found in every block of a slum, a house that constantly has people passing in and out at all hours of the night, that neighbors invariably assume is evil but a house that they only have the most pleasant dealings with. Somewhere on the street, behind another door, a tambourine thumped and rang, thumped and hissed, chimed and hissed. He banged his fist on the dented metal door.

"Rachel," he shouted when the door cracked to reveal one of Rachel's large dark eyes. She closed the door and he heard her slide the chain off. Then she was in his arms, filling his whole body with the energy of her warm supple strength. As she led him into the dimly lighted front room he noticed her curly hair was fixed in a new manner with combs holding it in a bun on top of her head. She wore a loose wool skirt and white blouse. On the floor, couches and beds and in sleeping bags were denim-clad, bearded men.

"Don't hug me so hard," she said, frowning at him and touching her breasts.

"How's Dan?" Jacob asked, following Rachel into a small bedroom. On one wall was a sketch of Rachel looking forward and upward in a religious pose, on the other was a drawing of a group of Negroes who listened to a fellow who rose above the crowd and seemed to be cajoling and beseeching the others in the crowd. The unknown abysms from which each of the souls in the picture came to that particular piece of ground were suggested by cubist style and unusual choice of color.

"There he is," Rachel said, pointing to a silently sleeping baby in a crib. "Dan Sekou Nothing. Hello Mr. Nothing." She placed her head close to the crib.

"Please don't," Jacob said.

"Do you think it'll be cold in Washington?" Rachel asked.

"Very cold this winter."

"You'll be the first black Congressman from this state in a hundred years."

"I haven't won yet."

"You will. Anyway, whether you do or don't we're all going to Washington to protest or celebrate."

Jacob studied the sleeping face of the child. He didn't sleep like the typical ghetto child with a frown on his brow, tossing and turning with fearful dreams, but instead slept peacefully.

"Have you been feeding Dan the formula?"

"No. But I get a little goat's milk for him sometimes."

Jacob reached into his pocket and drew out a fistful of bills and pushed them into her hand. She looked directly into his face and seemed to search for something with her penetrating eyes. Jacob knew that there was something that he, a respected community leader, and she, a member of a revolutionary movement, had to say to one another that would be different than anything any two people who had created a black child had said before; something like—our child will have a history and a land to call his own; but he was silent.

"He will have a father, won't he, Jacob?" Rachel said, softly hugging him.

"Our next Congressman," said Curtingham (Curt) Korny, Jesse's friend, a tall fellow with a moustache who spoke looking down his broad black nose as though he balanced invisible spectacles as Jacob entered the kitchen where several people sat around a table. Curt wore a black suitcoat over a white shirt, black-and-white checked, continental-cut highwater pants and beaten down brown shoes.

Also seated at the table was Van Cliffords, a man who had missed his calling and was at his best when selling something. Cliffords was clothed in a leather vest which covered a black shirt stuck down in black tight levis and on his bare feet were thong sandals. His long red hair and reddish tinged skin were shockingly offset by his blue eyes. Ray Stokes, agitator and apostle of the Third Testament that hasn't been written yet, wore a "Mao" suit imported from England and low-cut cowboy boots. Then there was Brad Wilson, the printer who had eaten and slept in the print shop during the campaign, grinding out leaflets, pamphlets and posters, and who wore a World War II army campaign jacket over an African Buba, an old pair of blue serge pants and sneakers.

Jesse entered the kitchen wiping his hands on a towel. "Jesse!" Jacob shouted. "How'd you . . . glad to see you out."

"We bailed the bastard out," Cliffords said. "Money we could've used for literature or tents."

"Watch your mouth," Jesse said.

"Perhaps Jacob has some idea about a problem we were discussing."

"Yeah," Brad Wilson said.

"I think we not only got to build institutions," Cliffords said, "but we got to be willing to defend them."

"No, that's not the issue," Curtingham said. The tall West Indian spoke with a slight British accent. "A cop at a voting poll picks a fight with a brother and we shoot him. Then we'd have to fight the Sheriff's office. If we win then we'd have to fight the state troopers, then we'd have to fight the national guard. If we beat the guard, then we face the U. S. army and finally NATO and Russia. And the whole white world, simply because we opposed one white man. So we have the choice of fighting and dying or not fighting and perishing unheralded with no one ever asking, who are those people? Where did they come from?"

"Curtingham's an expert in the use of the false dilemma," Jesse said. "Either this way or that way when actually it's neither way."

"How do you feel?" Jacob asked, looking him over.

"Not bad," he said, flinching when Jacob touched his wrist.

At all stages of the campaign Jacob had relied heavily upon Jesse. When the whites changed the places of registration for voters, Jesse had found them and had lines of Negroes waiting for them to open the next day. When they said there would only be one day of registration a month, Jesse had a lawyer successfully sue the registrar. When the shootings and evictions started, Jesse got the FBI to come into the area. Jesse had nationally known leaders who came into the district speak in Jacob's behalf. Somehow Jesse had gotten hold of a sample registration test and a sample ballot and had copies printed and circulated.

"You're overlooking one thing," Ray Stokes said. "And that is the Man has a plan to wipe out all you niggers. A hundred years ago he started depopulating Africa, America and Australia and populating these continents with his own race. Now he's been fairly successful in that—and that's because he's developed kill power—he's now turning to the yellow people . . ."

Jacob had noticed that to Stokes it didn't matter what was said; he knew what had to be done and did it. Discussions to him seemed to be games played for the sake of playing and shooting the breeze. But on the other hand, Stokes seemed to know that at times the silliest words between men are impor-tant, that they can be matters of life and death. Stokes moved faster than his words, his actions rather than his words being the final definition of himself. He moved with his words slow sounds trailing behind him for the dull to master. When he argued, it was to justify his action and his arguments were full of the traps and snares that he could manage to weave. He would use the maze of history to lead a listener's thought to his present position. He knew that for most people the past and the present are one and the same, the mistakes of yesterday being the mistakes of today. The fusion of yesterday's fact and today's hope into myth formed binding and clever entrapments for supporters as well as enemies. Stokes was the kind of man, Jacob thought, who would try anything once. And Stokes, Jacob had come to learn during the months they'd worked together on the campaign, had been in prison admittedly at least twenty times and once had been arrested upon four occasions in one day; each time bond was posted, he'd been arrested again on a new charge.

Stokes tuned a small portable radio in on a hoarse distorted voice that was saying, ". . . if you're born again you cannot sin. If only this was a Christian nation. If only I could tell you folks that even the leaders . . ."

"That's Reverend Hosea Gilsby," Rachel said.

"What's on the news?" Wilson asked.

"The press is distorting everything we're doing," Jacob said.

"Did you see that article in the *Times?* How'd they find out that the folks out at Tent City are armed if they didn't hear it from one of us?" Jesse asked.

"The Klan could've told them," Curt said.

"It's the white liberals you all so willing to talk to all the time," Cliffords said.

"The coverage in the European press is good," Stokes said.

"Did you see the articles Jeanne sent from Paris when that correspondent got killed during the school crisis?" Curt asked.

"Man, they tore at this country's throat."

Stokes tuned the radio in on "The Funky Momma Blues" and started dancing. Rachel joined him. Cliffords began dancing alone, a dance of the soul in harmony with the body, hands, eyes and arms striking religious poses never recorded by a painter, movements of the stomach and hips that spoke of love for his own black self.

Jesse moved close to Jacob and said, "The rally's all set for tomorrow. We've contacted all the churches, pamphlets have been sent all through the town and we've even forced one radio station to announce it."

"Fine. Sounds like you did your usual efficient job," Jacob said.

Within Jacob there had always been a problem of how much of himself to reveal to others, how much to make vulnerable. How much of his training could he display in an impoverished community and how much of his folksiness could he display when in the presence of entrenched white power. But with the young men and women in the movement he'd found no such problem and to a degree already felt the freedom that he sought. Because he'd rarely put forth any one part of his nature he'd not developed the strength he could if constantly challenged and tested. When pressed to the wall, he'd changed personalities like overcoats. The only thing that didn't change was the color of his skin. He was forever black, black in a white man's nation.

13

Roots

JACOB'S PLANS TO RETURN to his office by two didn't work out. When he got to his office at three he found there an infuriated matron who'd come to see him about "nature problems" and a farmer whose hand had been caught in a mower earlier in the week and was dangerously infected.

By six o'clock Jacob was once more at his desk, receiving no one, taking no calls, sipping vodka and tonic, trying to piece together the puzzle of his past. Before him was placed the large family bible in whose aging pages there were written the major sorrows and ceremonies of his family. His mother had read to him from it but always forbade him to open it. An ancient flower was pressed between the thick leather cover and the front pages where written in gold leaf were the words *The Holy Bible.*

On the next page, written in bold old letters, was the word *Marriages* and under that was written in script: "1865, Moja and Odetta; 1889, John L. Ricks and Tessy Grace; 1900, Sarah Ricks and Obediah Gittens; 1905, John Ricks, Jr., and Ella Derby; 1907, John Ricks, Jr., and Rita Frailty; 1919, . . . ; 1928, Anne Ricks and Aubrey Blue; 1955, Jacob Blue and Leah Labar." There were a few blank pages and then the pages for *Births:* "1866, . . . ; 1867, . . . ; 1880, Sarah Ricks; 1883, Peter Ricks; 1884, Al Ricks; 1885, John Ricks, Jr.; 1901 . . . ; 1904, . . . ; 1906, Anne Ricks; 1921, Dora Moor; 1925, Nat Blue; 1930, Jacob Blue."

Several pages further Jacob found listed the *Deaths:* "1865, . . . ; 1869, . . . ; 1870 . . . ; 1890, Peter Ricks was taken; 1902, . . . ; 1903, . . . ; 1910, Al Ricks; 1920, John L. Ricks; 1929, Aubrey Blue."

Jacob tore a corner off a page and placed the acrid-tasting paper on his tongue. Jacob asked himself who these people were. Faceless images of tall, strong people who'd surrounded him in his youth came back to him. This was the same bible that Grace and before him Grace's father had used to read the scripture when they came calling upon his sickly mother. This was the same bible that his mother had warned Grace against opening to Genesis. They had obeyed her, understanding it to be the crank of an old woman. He would see.

Jacob carefully studied the pages of Genesis developing its destroyer-builder God and then on the page where Genesis 22 was found there was preserved a yellow newsclipping.

MATCHEZ, MISS., APR. 24—The body of Aubrey Blue, a Negro who was implicated in the Jackson murder by Lewis Holmes, was found swinging from the limb of a persimmon tree within a mile and quarter of Matchez, Miss., early today. Before death was allowed to end the suffering of the Negro, his ears were cut off . . .

Jacob read again: . . . his ears were cut off . . . his . . . his ears were cut off . . . his ears were cut off . . . his ears were cut off . . . his ears were cut off . . . his ears were cut off . . .

. . . cut off and the small finger of his left hand was severed at the second joint. Those trophies were in Matchez yesterday on display at Lorchman's General Store. On the chest of the Negro was a piece of blood-stained paper, attached by an ordinary pin. On one side of this paper was written: "We must protect our ladies."

The other side of the paper contained a warning to the Negroes of the neighborhood. It read as follows: "Beware all darkies! You will be treated the same way."

Before being lynched, Blue was given a chance to confess to the misdeeds of which the mob supposed him to be guilty, but he protested his innocence to the last. Three times the noose was placed around his neck and the Negro was drawn up off the ground; three times he was let down with a warning that death was in store for him should he fail to confess his complicity in the Cranford murder. Three times Blue proclaimed his innocence until, weary of useless torturing, the mob pulled on the rope and tied the end around the slender trunk of the persimmon tree. Not a shot was fired. Blue was strangled to death.

The lynching of Aubrey Blue was not accomplished without a desperate effort on the part of his employer to save his life. The man who pleaded for him is Major W.W. Nicholson, an ex-state senator, and one of the most distinguished citizens of Coweta County. He did all in his power to prevent the lynching of the Negro and did not discontinue his efforts until he had been assured by the leaders of the mob that the Negro would be taken to jail at Fairburn. One mile from the spot where this promise was made, Blue was hanged. The Negro was a tenant on the plantation of Major Nicholson. When Lewis Holmes, the murderer of Alfred Cranford and the assailant of his wife, made his confession immediately prior to his burning, he implicated Aubrey Blue, Holmes contending that he had been offered money by Blue to kill Cranford. It was known positively, however, that Holmes had made false statements in his last confession, and many of those who aided in his burning were disposed to disregard his statements in regard to Blue.

About 15 men went to the plantation of Major Nicholson late Sunday night and took Blue from his little cabin in the woods, and left his wife to wait and weep over the fate she knew was in store for the Negro. Her cries aroused Major Nicholson, and that sturdy old man followed the lynchers in his buggy, accompanied by his son, Samuel Nicholson, determined to save, if possible, the life of his plantation darkey, it is reported. They overtook the lynchers with their victim at Matchez, and then ensued, with only the moonlight to brighten their faces of the grim men, a weird and dramatic scene. Aubrey Blue was halted directly opposite the telegraph office. The noose was adjusted around his neck and the end of the rope was thrown over a tree. Blue was told he had a chance before dying to confess his complicity in the crime. He replied: "I have told you all I know, gentlemen. You can kill me if you wish, but I know nothing to tell."

The Negro's life might have been ended then but

for the arrival of Major Nicholson, who leaped from his buggy and asked for a hearing. He asked the crowd to give the Negro a chance for his life and said, "Gentlemen, this Negro is innocent. Holmes said Aubrey had promised to give him $20 to kill Alfred Cranford, and I don't believe Aubrey had $20 since he has been on my place. He has never done any of you any harm; I want you to promise me that you will turn him over to the bailiff of this town that he may be given a hearing. I do not ask you to liberate him. Hold him for the courts." The mob replied that Blue had inflamed the Negroes in the neighborhood and had a bad reputation, having run away from Eastpoint several years ago. Major Nicholson reminded the mob that the Negro had voluntarily told of having seen Holmes on the night of the murder. One of the mob replied that Blue had done this in the cunningness of his guilt to establish his own innocence.

There were some, however, who agreed with Major Nicholson and, after a discussion, a vote was taken which was supposed to mean life or death to Aubrey Blue. The vote to let him live was unanimous. Major Nicholson then retired to some distance, and the mob was preparing to send Blue in a wagon to Fairburn when a member of the mob cried out: "We have got him here, let's keep him." This aroused the mob and a messenger was sent to advise Major Nicholson to leave Matchez for his own good, but the old man was not frightened. He drew himself up and said emphatically: "I have never before been ordered to leave a town, and I am not going to leave this one." And then the Major, lifting up his hand to give his words force, said to the messenger: "Tell them the muscles in my legs are not trained for running, tell them I have stood the fire and heard the whistles of minié balls from a

thousand Yankee rifles, and I am not frightened by
this crowd." Major Nicholson was not molested.
Then, with the understanding that Aubrey Blue was
to be delivered to the jailer at Fairburn, Major Nicholson saw the Negro he had pleaded for led off to his
death.

The mob took the Negro to a grove near the home
of Marshall Clayton of Matchez and again the noose
was adjusted. He was hauled off the ground, but was
let down to allow him to confess. He refused to do so,
and the lynchers were about to haul him up again
when the son of Marshall Clayton came upon the
scene and asked that the lynching should not occur
near his father's home. The Negro was then taken to
the yard in the rear of Dr. S. W. Heller's home and
tied up to a persimmon tree and left hanging. A coro-
ner's jury held an inquest over the body Monday afternoon and returned the usual verdict—death at the
hands of parties unknown. Another mob is hunting
the county for Albert Sewell, who has made himself
obnoxious by remarks concerning the treatment given
the Negroes by the whites.

Jacob felt as though someone had grabbed him by his balls.
His lower abdomen was queasy, he was perspiring and he trembled fearfully as he strode to his mother's room, the yellowed
paper clasped in his hand. "Mother."

"Come in. What's troubling you, son?"

Widow Sanders helped prop Anne up with pillows and sat
back down in a rocking chair beside the bed.

"Is this true?"

The two octogenarians looked at the paper in his hand. "So,
you found it?"

"In the Bible. Genesis."

"I . . ."

"What? How did . . ."

"There are some things better not said . . ."

"Not this. I got to know. Everything . . ." he said, wishing his mother were alone.

"There was some rapin' and some killin' . . ."

"Blood to the north, fire to the south," Widow Sanders said. "I seen it in my dreams."

"You hush," Anne said.

"Was Aubrey a rapist?" Jacob said, breathing deeply and regaining his composure. He sat down in a soft, deep armchair.

"Now remember this. And take some of the burning from my heart to yours. When you were younger I didn't think you could live knowing. But looks to me like you knows too well how to survive . . ."

"What do you mean?" Jacob asked. Usually Jacob could only stand Widow Sander's presence for a moment because he was constantly reminded by the strange objects on the string around her neck of her practice as an Obi woman, midwife and charmer. But somehow, now, her presence was comforting.

"Miss Cranford like men. Some women like dat. Can't hep it. Lewis Holmes and Aubrey was workin' in the yard o' Cranford. Sam Nicholson, he come by while the old man was out. Old man caught Sam wid Miss Cranford. Well, Mr. Cranford, he quick pulled down his axe from the doorway like to kill Mr. Sam. But Mr. Sam grab it from Cranford and kill him wid dat axe. Lewis an' my Aubrey see the whole thing."

"That's why Lewis and Aubrey were killed?"

"Lewis and Aubrey went to their homes scared o' what dey saw. Mr. Sam and Mrs. Cranford got up that story and the mob came for Lewis. Lewis told the white folk about Aubrey bein' there. Well it weren't long before Major Nicholson told us that if'n Aubrey didn't say nothin' about his son, he would try and get Aubrey freed. He said if'n we come out talkin' crazy, he'd side wid the mob and then both o' us would be lost."

Jacob closed his eyes, clenched his fist and breathed deeply.

"Easy now, son."

"No," Jacob said.

"Old Major Nicholson, he were a good man and hepped me."

"How can you say he's good, momma?"

"He give me money to hep raise you."

"He's evil. All he was doing was covering up his crimes," Jacob proclaimed.

"He wanted us to stay on his plantation. Begged me to so's he could take care o' us."

"So's you could starve," said Widow Sanders. "The land we fought the Indians for, cleared the stumps from and planted, he decided to take and grow trees and cattle."

"He begged us to stay on the land," Anne said.

"And starve to death while he gave us Thanksgiving turkeys and Christmas baskets," Widow Sanders said in her rasping voice.

Jacob would never remember how he got from his mother's room downstairs to his study for his mind was charged with anger. In his desk he found a snub-nosed .38 and placed it in his pocket where it lay heavily on his leg. Where, he wondered, do the lies begin? When they said slavery ended? When slavery of his people became popular in the 1800s? But more terrible than the public lies were the private lies whispered between mother and son, lovers, brothers, and whispered to oneself.

Jacob could hear screams and melodramatic voice-sounds from the bedroom TV signifying that Leah had not missed her daily Soap opera. Jacob paced the room wondering. Here he was, a freak of mankind who had been taught to feel within himself certain sentiments that would not allow him to live, in any sense, as a man. He felt hollow for he was distrustful of the beliefs others had forced upon him. He did not really understand or even remember much of his own experience. He wasn't sure that his mother had told him the truth and wished he could remember his childhood; who he played with and who the adults were around him. But then he had accepted people without regard for names, titles or genealogies.

He heard someone open the front door and hurried out of the study. "Jacob," Frailty said, meeting him in the hallway. Taking note of Frailty's outfit of tweed, patent-leather shoes, fuzzy-looking hat with a small red feather, an obscene ruffled formal shirt and green socks, Jacob walked past him and locked the door. Walking into the study after Jacob, Frailty asked, "Paranoic?"

"Any Negro who isn't paranoic is like a boxer who doesn't duck punches."

"Aren't you going to congratulate me?"

"For what?"

"Haven't you heard I've been named deputy sheriff?"

"Can you fix parking tickets?"

"I don't know. I need a drink," he said, flopping heavily into a chair.

"You're the first, huh?"

"Yeah. It don't mean much."

"How's the housing committee?" Jacob asked, taking some bourbon and a shot glass from his liquor cabinet.

"I gave the seed money to bind the contract to Nicholson. He's in Washington and will be back tomorrow."

"It's not illegal, is it?"

"No. You always got ta grease the palm of them big boys. It's not that they need the money. No. It's more like they wants the gesture."

Jacob had always admired Frailty's ability to handle whites and wondered what the source of his talent was—his father, school, the army, his money?

Setting piles of documents on the table Frailty directed Jacob's hand to the line for his signature. Jacob's signature would appear along with Grace, Strop, Frailty, Nicholson and Nelson on the contracts.

"I'm putting off painting the house in order to get in on

this," Jacob said. "With Broom and Fletcher as architects, Hansen as builder and Reverend Grace's church as sponsor, this should work."

"It's good you're on the ground floor. When this breaks, everyone'll want in. Even my pa will stop calling me a tomfool and try to buy or steal shares."

"You know Bernard's going to clean up."

"What-da-ya mean?" Frailty asked.

"He'll loan the building companies money to buy materials, his bank is part of a syndicate that'll buy and sell bonds. We need our own bank and our own building company."

"Maybe later," Frailty said. "First things first."

"I keep them for my special guests," Jacob said, offering Frailty a puritano from his humidor.

Frailty wet it with his lips so it would burn smoothly, bit off the tip and spit it casually on the floor, and lit up.

"What do you think of this?" Jacob said, pulling the pistol from his pocket.

"Beautiful," Frailty said.

"Thirty-eight."

"Good. Easy to buy ammunition. Say, you ain't a member of the minutemen?" Frailty laughed.

"No, but I think I may need it before the week's over."

"Going to shoot your wife?"

"Wrong again."

"Seriously, Jacob. This is one of the first signs that you have the sense that you were born with. You better keep that thing near you and loaded."

Jacob stared Frailty in the eyes for a moment, then slapped him on the back and walked him to the door where they parted in the yellow light cast by the hall chandelier. That kind of advice from that particular source was serious indeed.

The sound of the TV filled the house. Jacob climbed into his car and sped into the Mississippi night. Finding the campaign office dark and closed he parked and walked down the street toward the light and noise coming from Fats's Pool Hall.

"Hey man," said a fellow in a black shirt and green pants.

"Baby," said a big fellow with a leather jacket, slapping Jacob on the shoulder.

"How're you doing," Jacob said, shaking hands with everyone.

"They think they own the place," Fats said, walking toward Jacob and throwing his hands in the air. "I might as well go out of business. They don't start until twelve. But half my business has walked out the door waiting for them to play."

Jacob looked at the little bandstand in the back room where several musicians lethargically went about setting up their instruments. Doc seemed to be asleep on the bass, Charlie thumped at the bass pedal and Dan fiddled with the electric amplifier hooked up to the piano. Jacob waved to two women at the bar and a couple of men seated by the jukebox and sat down with Rachel, Curt and Jesse. There were a couple of strange white men in the place. Jacob had seen one of them before but couldn't remember where.

"Jacob, we closed up to do a little politicking in the bars," Rachel said.

"So I see," he said, looking about for a waitress.

Jacob couldn't help overhearing the loud-talking women at the bar. "You look nice, darling," Freddie, Fats's wife, told Fannie. Freddie stood behind the bar opening beer cans.

"Oh, do you like it?" Fannie said, touching her wig with long graceful, carefully manicured fingernails. Fannie had on the latest mode dress and had managed to focus the stares of all the men in the place on her.

"Hey baby," a fellow said.

"Yes sugar," Fannie replied.

"Come 'ere and let me have about five pounds of the sweet Missidamnsippi meat you got there."

"You better get out of here," Freddie said.

Carol, Alice, Vivian and Fats stared in the bar mirror at Fannie.

"Anyone of you mothers touch my new wig there's goin' a be a fight," Fannie said jokingly but with a bit of challenge. "Buy me a drink," Jacob heard her ask the white fellow seated near her.

"Sure Fannie," he said. "Freddie, give Fannie what she wants."

"Who's that?" Jacob asked.

"Some white faggot," Curt said. "Or else he's The Man." Curt, Jesse, Jacob and Rachel watched the scene at the bar.

Fats moved down the bar to Fannie. "You seen them musicians?" he asked her. "They think I'm crazy. They'll see how crazy I am when it comes time to pay them. They think they smart. When they come in tonight they tells me their wrist-watch—the poor sons-o'-bitches only got one between them—they says their watch is slow. And I like a fool looks at it. And sure enough they had it turned back."

"What do you want to drink?" Freddie asked Fannie.

"A beer, honey."

"What do you think of my remodeling?" Fats said, sweeping his hand around.

Jacob looked around the place but could find little difference from what it had been the last time he was there.

"Just great, honey. How much the drinks going up?" Fannie asked.

The people at the bar and Jesse, Curt, Jacob and those within hearing laughed.

"Ain't nothing going up," Fats said. "This here's a service to the customers." He laid his hand on Fannie's shoulder and said, "Of course there's going to be a cover charge . . ."

"Ha, you're something else."

Vivian watched Fannie and Fats with narrowed eyes. Vivian's hair and dress looked like that of the "flapper girls" of that time. Her hair was slicked down about her head like a boy's. A tight-fitting striped sweater added to the effect. As Fats left Fannie's side to speak to his wife who was on the phone at the other end of the bar, Vivan glided up to her.

"Listen, bitch," she said. "You leave my man alone."

"I'll talk to who I want to talk to, darling," Fannie said.

Vivian reached up and snatched the red wig from Fannie's head, leaving her natural, uncombed hair standing straight up. Fannie threw her beer on Vivian and before anyone could grab her smashed the glass on her head.

Grabbing her head in her hands Vivian started screaming, "She's trying to kill me."

Fats grabbed Fannie and wrestled her into a chair in the corner. Freddie led Vivian into the ladies' room.

"Friday night," Curt laughed.

"But you know the truth is that serious crimes, killings and robbings have almost stopped in the ghetto," Jesse said. "The same thing happened in Belzoni and even in Jackson when the movement was organized there."

Jacob noted that the fellow at the bar kept pushing his glasses to the top of his nose. "I've seen that white fellow somewhere before," Jacob said.

"He's studying us," Rachel said. "He says he's going to write a book about social change in a Southern town. He's been in the office a couple of times."

"I'll tell you who he is," Jesse said. "He comes in here looking for strong young black fellows to take home with him." Curt waved his arms at Fats. When Fats made his way to the table through a growing crowd, he whispered in his ear. The music had started and the people were packing in. Fats returned with a bottle. When the band started to play, Jacob noticed that one of the white fellows in the place was on the bandstand with a golden horn, marching along with the piano, doing a tune called "Stereophonic." Then they hit "Moanin'." Everything was played at a blurring speed.

"I sure like this down-home stuff rather than some of the pseudo-tinsel jazz exponents."

"Oh, hell, here we go," Jesse said.

"That's right," Curt said pouring another round of drinks. "What you got there may be rough, but it's better than that stuff that's been rounded out, cooled off and eased out of what's happening."

The band leader then pushed his group to play "Lady Bird," moving from one up-tempo, flighty piece to another. "He's going to kill his drummer," Curt observed.

"I'm afraid I can't get over Louie Armstrong or Duke Ellington," Jacob said.

"They're myths," Curt shouted above the band. "Only musicians like Archie Shep, Sun Ra, Sunny Murray, and Andrew Hill are able to inform the masses what jazz is about. Have some more liquor," Curt urged Jacob.

"I better order some food," Jacob said. The thought of a juicy steak, or some chicken gumbo or barbecued pork ribs made him salivate and his stomach growled. "A steak," he called to Fats. While he was ordering Curt and Jesse were arguing over the relative merits of Count and Duke.

Jacob could smell the steak cooking in the kitchen and before it reached his table he'd eaten it a thousand times in his mind. He cut a couple of pieces off and doused them with Worchestershire Sauce, ketchup, meat tenderizer and salt and pepper. As he started to place the meat in his mouth a rough, weathered black hand reached past his shoulder and picked the other piece of meat from his plate. Everyone at the table was silent and stone-still. Jacob turned around and recognized Old Man Gittens' cold, oblivious face. "Sit down," Jacob asked him.

"No. I just wants a little taste, Mr. Jacob."

Jesse found another chair and placed it near Mr. Gittens. Jacob pushed the plate of meat and potatoes over to him. "Go ahead," he said.

Gittens gobbled away as though he would die if he stopped

eating. Finally the plate was wiped completely clean with a piece of bread. Gittens had the odor of a wino about him. It was the smell of digested alcohol, vomited up or coming out of the pores of his skin, his breath and urine. "What's happening with you and your family?" Jacob asked.

Gittens was silent.

"Can we help you?" Rachel asked.

"Freedom. Liberty. Sheeeeeeeit," Mr. Gittens said.

Perspiration poured down his face which twisted with some strange derangement fearful to see. "What the hell you people think you trying to do? Damn it. Freedom. Sheeeeeeit."

"Just tell us what's wrong," Rachel said.

"Sheeeeeeit," Gittens said.

"Okay, brother," Curt said. "You're a big man. You've got your ideas. You tell us what we should do if you don't like the freedom bit."

"Make a decent living, damn it," Gittens said. "Get an honest job. Work like the rest of us."

"And what have you accomplished as a respectable laborer, brother?" Curt asked.

Rachel seemed intimidated by the man, Jacob confused and Jesse saddened. Suddenly they noticed that their table had become the center of attraction of the bar. "All right, brother," Jesse said.

"And I ain't no brother of you folk. Where the hell do you get the money to run around the country causing trouble and beating the court cases against you?"

"By having faith," Curt said.

"Bull. Black Power, Nitty-gritty. Freedom. Sheeeit."

"Some time when you're feeling better we'll have to talk at length," Jacob said.

Looking up from his empty plate Gittens said, "Sheeeit." And then he rose and disappeared into the bathroom with a man in a long black ragged coat and gold-rimmed eyeglasses.

Curt got up and found something to laugh about with Fannie and the white fellow at the bar. Vivian stood in a corner glowering at Fannie, and Fats was "waltzing" around as though nothing had happened.

Jacob wondered where Gittens would fit into Jesse's ideas about the beautiful masses. He knew it would have been a crude move to throw that particular incident up in Jesse's face. After all, he could think too.

"That'll be ten dollars," Fats said, walking up to the table with pad in hand.

"What do you mean?" Jacob asked. "I only had a steak."

"The liquor," Fats said.

"Curt ordered that. Anyway, that's certainly not eight dollars."

"Curt ain't got no money." Fats almost sounded belligerent. Somehow Jacob felt out of sorts as though he were playing a totally unfamiliar role. "Now I got to get my money out o' someone. What's it goin' to be?"

Jacob counted out the money as Fats explained, "It cost two dollars for the set-up, the ice and juice." Jacob gave him a two-dollar tip. At times like that Jacob wondered how he would ever afford some of his friends.

Curt pushed through the crowd of drinkers, loiterers and dancers toward Jacob's table followed by Schneider.

"Schneider, this is Dr. Blue," he said.

Jacob shook Schneider's hard small hand and the thin, pale-faced man took a seat near Jacob. "How *do* your chances look?" Schneider asked.

"Very good," Jacob said. "If we can keep the white cemetery from voting." Everyone at the table laughed except Jesse who seemed shrouded tightly in hatred for the stranger. Jacob reached inside his coat and touched the cool metallic object that pressed against him.

"Do you mean there'll be a lot of cheating at the polls?" Schneider asked.

"Of course, don't you think so?" Jacob said.

"Who would organize such a thing? Doesn't Whiteman, your opponent, have the loyalty of enough whites to give you a good race?"

"Of course. But he wants a sure win."

"What do you think of the argument that Whiteman should stay in Congress because of the seniority he's built up?"

"I think the fact that Whiteman has become chairman of the Appropriations Committee through the seniority system is proof of the fallacy of the system. It obviously doesn't produce the best leadership."

Everyone at the table was quiet as they listened intently to Jacob and Schneider.

"Why haven't you solicited white support?"

"Why haven't they offered support?" Jacob asked.

"Do you mean to say you wait for support to walk through your front door?"

"I mean I don't ask people for support who haven't proven their loyalty or interest somehow. Do you think a lamb should seek the support of wolves?"

"Has the Justice Department been involved?" Schneider asked.

"Rose is singing," Jacob said, turning to watch the vocalist, seeming not to hear Schneider. Again he placed his hand on the comforting bulge at his side.

"I want to love you like nobody's loved you come rain or come shine . . . " she crooned, low and deep and soft.

"Nobody can sing like Rose," Jacob said. Everybody in the place stopped and listened to the large woman with the beautiful face in the spotlight, sing love songs, sorrow songs and snappy pop tunes. Not a glass clinked while she sang.

When the singing stopped and the hooting and clapping died down Schneider asked Jacob for an appointment. "Actually I'd like to watch you on Election Day. Travel around with you.

You see I'm writing an article on your movement for a national publication. A friend of mine who's editor of *Live* magazine commissioned me. You're making history, Jacob."

"We'll be moving pretty fast. Come to our headquarters Monday morning," Jacob said.

Schneider shook hands with everyone and went back to the bar to kid and joke with Fannie and Freddie.

"That faggot sure is nosey," Curt said. "Asked me to introduce him to you."

"And you did it," Jesse said. "Monday I don't want that fellow poking around."

"He seems sympathetic," Rachel said.

"Sympathy is just asking for details," Curt said.

Through the web that the liquor had placed on his face Jacob saw Gittens going into the bathroom once more with another derelict, the musicians pounded out "Satin Doll," their minds lost behind glassy, dope-clouded eyes, a few U.S. Marines came in buying drinks for the women at the bar, girls in gay-looking clothes hustled in and out of the room with young men, and a group of girls ran happily to the ladies' room to smoke or to play with each other. The girls were atrocious, running their hands all over each other and dancing together. Jacob excused himself and, feeling terribly ill, drove Rachel home and then headed toward his house. He was warmed that chilly night by the memory of Rachel's parting kiss, lips softer than velvet and arms with the black strength of a panther, the simple smell of freshly laundered clothes and oiled hair. And in the back of his mind was the uncomfortable feeling of guilt for Gittens. None of us should be trapped into Gittens' position, he thought; better to be dead. He wondered how it would be facing his mother knowing the truth about his hateful but very Southern origin.

Jacob was happy. The trip to Fats's had accomplished one thing he'd hoped: the thousand thoughts buzzing around his head were turning into a silent burning feeling. Just as the night outside the car was full of flighty bats sweeping about the dark sky to catch insects on the wing, so his mind had been full of thoughts seeking morsels of truth. But all of the questions were gone and all that mattered was the hum of the road and the memory of "Satin Doll" and an ironic burning in him that made him laugh and cry out in the same breath.

III

14

Saturday, the Campaign

"CLICK. Do you have surplus liver acid, folks? Well take
Swamp Root and feel yourself once again. Start those liver acids
moving with Swamp Root.

"Now for the wonderful WZNY news. Monday four hundred thousand men and women from across the state will go to
the polls to exercise their right to vote for local, state, and
federal officials. In an interesting development in the seventh
district, the Party will be challenged by a Negro independent.
Whiteman, the regular party candidate says he expects little

opposition from Jacob Blue, the Matchez Negro who opposes him . . . "

"You awake, Jacob?" Leah asked.

" . . . and now that we've heard the news it's time for the Reverend Hosea Gilsby. "I pray that Almighty God bless your mind with a prayer of deliverance. A prayer of deliverance is our only hope and salvation. There are some of us Matchez folks who would seek violent means of change. But when you stir up a hornet's nest you have to expect to be stung. Only prayer will bring about . . . "

Jacob tuned to a station where a gospel group sang, "Satan, we're going to tear your kingdom down . . . "

"You getting up?" Jacob asked.

"For what? I'm sooo tired."

"You're not going to help campaign today?"

"I told you what I think of your foolishness. Only psychotics worry about the welfare of the whole wide world like you do. You ought to worry about your own business. You don't like to think about those things do you? How will we eat? Supposing we have a child?"

"Why should we be rich when everyone around us is poor?"

"You're crazy. I'm not talking about being rich, just living."

"You are going to vote Monday morning with me?"

"Shessy, Casey and I are going downtown in the afternoon after everything is calmed down. You ought to wait until afternoon, Jacob. It won't be safe in the morning. By afternoon any disturbances will be settled one way or another." Leah flopped over on her stomach and closed her eyes.

Jacob quickly dressed, reheated coffee made the night before and poured it into a tall glass with cream and sugar—a habit Leah found particularly obnoxious. He glanced through the newspaper only reading the headlines. The main story was about the war, telling of glorious victories; the story given second billing on the front page was about a liquor raid; one of the main articles near the center of the page was about the political race, repeating the simple lines established by the candidates early in the race and spiced with revelation of a new scandal. On the sixth page was the news of the Negro community; deaths, births and accidents that you found out about soon enough anyway. He threw the paper into the garbage after first carefully removing the Negro page and society page for Leah. A car rumbled into the drive and Jacob ran to the window to peek out between the curtains. It was Curt and Jesse in the sound truck.

Slamming the screen, which he'd forgotten to take down for the winter, they entered the kitchen. Both men had tired red eyes.

"We been out in the rurals talking to people all morning," Jesse said.

"Stokes is downtown now working. You ready?"

"I've got to take some steps today to deal with the health problem at Tent City," Jacob said.

"I thought you were going to do that yesterday," Jesse said.

"A whole lot of other stuff came up," Jacob said.

Jacob found the job at Tent City immensely enjoyable. The people were cooperative and embarrassed him showing their gratitude. He knew, however, that he'd done nothing, for in the long run the Tent City families would succumb to the same diseases and deficiencies as other people in the community. Mrs. Rowe avoided Jacob, which disturbed him. But they finished quickly and headed back to town.

Jesse took the driver's wheel. Curt turned on the record player attached through a maze of wires to the loudspeaker on top of the truck. Blasting from the loudspeaker as they drove down Mangrum Street was the big "J. B." Dancing on the sidewalks as they drove past were schoolgirls, people waiting for buses and those milling around the barber shop, candy stores and gas stations. Old men, infants, housewives, schoolchildren, workers all stopped to dance to the music usually reserved for dances and parties. Parking the truck that had conspicuous BLUE FOR CONGRESS signs on its side, Jacob, Curt and Jesse jumped out.

When the crowd was large and happy a police car screeched to a stop at the edge of the crowd. "Here they are," Curt said. "Right on time." Jesse smiled. Jacob grabbed a mike attached to the loudspeaker. The music stopped as he said, "Look at those cops."

The street suddenly became a stage. The police and Jacob were actors, and the crowd of hundreds of critical black faces were the audience. But unlike most audiences, this one would feel and could be deadly in its judgment. "Did they come to protect us? Do they come when we are cheated in the grocery store? Do they come when the rent collector forces us to pay higher rents in the slums than they do in the white sections of town? Am I right or wrong, brother?" Jacob spoke directly to a fellow in fisherman's boots.

"You right. You right," the fellow said.

"We got to stop the cops beating heads and insulting us."

"You right, brother."

"Preach."

"Now I don't want to hear nobody talk who isn't registered. And if you aren't registered to vote go on down to the court- house and register so's you can vote next time."

Ending his talk, Jacob went to the truck and started the record turning. Some folks stood about deep in thought. Others began dancing. Getting back into their car and driving a block away the police stopped and watched.

At Water and Chestnut Streets Jacob spotted another crowd. "There's Stokes's people," Jesse said.

The two crowds joined and the people danced in the streets and shouted as they urged others along the side of the road to join in. The police directed traffic past the block.

Jacob watched and felt that he would be satisfied with his campaign if people only voted, whether he won or not. For in the past only a handful of rich black people voted and those votes, the votes of Strop, Grace, and Frailty, were only symbols of status. Whether or not he won, the fact that people were getting together, talking and doing things for themselves—this at least was some accomplishment. He could remember when NAACP meetings were conducted in secret and the six successive presidents of the Mississippi chapter had been assassinated.

Coffee cups strewn about his campaign headquarters by red-eyed workers added to the despairing, desolate appearance of the old building on Pearl Street that housed the office on the third floor.

Rachel busied herself sweeping around people with a makeshift broom of rushes tied to a stick. Males and females who'd come to work in the campaign all wore the same denim pants, army-surplus jackets and desert boots.

The radio was turned up full blast:

" . . . our man in Matchez, Al Keuter, reports that the Blue campaign may give us the first nigra Congressman from the state in one hundred years. The Negro doctor from the seventh district may win Monday's election our sample poll indicates. But a government spokesman says that there is concern on the part of the Justice Department that subversive elements may be finding a haven in the Blue campaign using the Negro candidate to further their own ends. A report from the Whiteman camp now. John Whiteman said in a special interview with QRNZ that he believes he will win and will continue to represent the people as their choice. He says that he has grave doubts about the legality of the Blue campaign. He says that Blue may not have complied with the state laws in qualifying as an Independent. Now for the international news. The war . . . "

"Turn that vile vituperation off," Curt said.

"Listen, I need a ride out to the airport," Jacob said. "I've got to get to New Orleans to a Medical Commission meeting on Nutritional Problems of the Poor."

"The meeting tonight . . . " Curt said.

"I'll be back."

Jacob, Curt and Jesse ran down the stairs to the truck. They barely made the morning flight.

IV

15

Puddin', Freed on Friday

THE QUEEN AND JACK LAY beside each other staring him in the face. "You can't go down now, baby. I got you covered. I'll kill your ass you go down now . . . "

"Man, you keep messing wid me, I'm goin' a put you out da back door."

"Motha, I wish you'd get it into your thick head that this kitty is mine . . . "

"It ain't no secret, baby, that you need a Heart. Here, man, look at the way these Queens spread. That's one Heart you ain't gettin'."

"I'll be damn, if you're going out. There, I'm hittin' your deuce-trey-four spread. If'n I remembers, the six is already buried in da pack."

Doc played the careful game that Puddin' would expect from a man of sixty years. Horse was getting reckless and wouldn't be in the game long. The corn whiskey they'd secretly brewed in the kitchen was getting the best of the fellow. Gabriel, who was sipping vanilla extract that day, was doing nicely but would soon lose all of the cigarettes he'd staked in the game. The four prisoners were taking a break in the exercise room before returning to the kitchen to fix food for the prisoners and the guards at the city jail.

Puddin' liked working in the kitchen because during the rest periods he could return to the recreation area to play cards and look at "The Secret Storm" TV drama. He also got a chance to steal food and other comforts from the kitchen. Before he'd started working in the kitchen he'd been constantly constipated by the breakfast of molasses, cornbread, bacon and coffee, the lunch of stew, collards, cornbread and coffee and the dinner of biscuits, mollasses, soup, and coffee or milk. And then he'd had to fight the others for a plate with some meat on it or else all he'd get was broth. But since he'd come to work in the kitchen where he could munch on an apple, a tomato or a piece of meat he'd given up the obsession that he was going to starve to death. His bowels started to move regularly and his shit no longer smelled the same as the food he was eating.

Puddin' looked past Horse and Gabriel, past Doc's white head to the cellblock gate. Standing behind the second gate was the Screw. The old son-of-a-bitch looks sad, Puddin' thought. What the hell he got to be sad about?

Horse looked up, saw the Screw and said, "Shit."

Puddin' could tell by the length of the shadows the bars on the windows made on the floor that it wasn't time to start cooking the midday meal. As usual, he'd been up at five to cook breakfast. His seven o'clock break was important to him. He was afraid the Screw was going to do something stupid like interrupt their card game. What the fuck did he want?

"How you boys doin'?" the Screw asked.

"Just lovely," Horse said under his breath.

Maybe the son-of-a-bitch had some candy or cigarettes he wants to sell, Puddin' thought. The MF couldn't o' come in there to chat.

"Puddin'," the Screw said officiously. "Come 'ere."

As Puddin' approached the gate separating the cells where they slept from the dining hall and rec pen, the gate slid open. "Pack your stuff," the Screw said.

"Where'm I goin', Mr. Hurst—sir?" Puddin' asked.

"You'll see. Get your stuff together. You got three minutes."

Puddin' grabbed the coat he'd had no reason to wear since his arrest and decided to leave the rest. The other guys could use the mirror, playing cards and cigarettes. He took the cigarettes from under his mattress and put them under the blanket on Gabriel's bunk. Gabriel had certainly treated him right, stealing food and cigarettes for him at every chance. He took the matchbox that held his pet water bug from the windowsill. He opened the box and dumped the startled black critter on the floor. The bug stood still for a second and then darted into a corner where it found a hole to crawl into. Puddin' had tied thread around the bug's leg and had enjoyed caring for it as he might have cared for his hunting dogs if he were home. He'd had another bug, called Blacky, before Sam, the one he'd just freed, but Doc had stomped it into the ground until it was just a glob of green and yellow juice. After the beating he'd given Doc, he never had any trouble from anyone about his hobby of keeping a bug in a matchbox.

Where were they taking him? He was supposed to have been released a month earlier. Perhaps he was being transferred to another jail or to the road gang. The life of a nigger wasn't shit. When they'd moved him from the work farm where he'd been picking cotton, he'd considered it a step toward freedom. Perhaps he'd been wrong. He'd had fantasy after fantasy about his dogs and being out hunting until he could hear the dogs bark, smell their coats wet from the dewy grass, feel the weight of his gun in his hands and the sting of the cold morning air in his nostrils.

His release was so simple, just walking to the door and leaving, that he wanted to rebel against it. His imprisonment didn't even mean enough for them to give him a good talking-to before he left. Perhaps they were just teasing him and would shoot him down or arrest him within a few blocks of the courthouse. But when he got to the Negro section of town he breathed easily and knew it was true—he was free at last.

Freedom was the road open before him and no reason to look back. The town was full of the usual morning milkman, paperboy, empty-street, lazy-dog sights. Frailty, the funeral businessman, was standing in front of his office in his crumpled clothes. He must have had a hard night. He didn't even see Puddin' walk cat-soft pass.

Puddin' felt light as the crisp morning air. Free at last. He was free at last. A big car reared through the street. Jumping out of the way, Puddin' caught sight of Miss Laura at the steering wheel. He wondered where "white folks" would be going in such a hurry that time of the morning. Probably up to no good.

He looked into one of the store windows that looked like sheets of ice along the street. The town was beginning to look like a big city, he thought. Studying his wavering image he decided his coat added a touch of dignity to his appearance. He'd managed to get fairly clean-shaven that morning. He peeked down over the bulge in his stomach to his shoes and was saddened by their cruddy look.

Down the street, near Fats's Pool Hall, he saw a couple of people and thought, get out of my way folks, don't you give me no conversation because I'm the meanest man that ever squatted between a pair of shoes. By the time he'd passed Fats's, where a light burned in the back, the people had disappeared. Crossing the tracks and walking among the tightly crammed shacks, Puddin' smelled the warm familiar odor of cooking fatback mixed with the smell of coal and wood stoves. More subtle was the odor of the rot that lay under the houses, mildewing and molding, for the bedsprings, mattresses, tables and furnishings of the people who lived and died in the neighborhood before the present occupants lay in garbage heaps upon which new dwellings had been built. The garbage made Puddin' think of the warning to the Hebrew children in Nehemiah not to build Jerusalum's walls on rubbish.

Entering the lane near his home he could hear Tina calling "Bocat. That boy waste mo' time." He hurried past a bunch of startled, frightened-looking children in the front room and, looking like a man of the road with his hair respectably graying, Puddin' walked straight for the kitchen.

"Paw's here," Dot yelled from the front room.

"You just tell that man he better keep walkin'," Tina yelled. "He better not put his convict feets in dis do'." Sensing his presence Tina plucked a pot of water from the stove. She turned and the pot shot across the room.

"Yeeeeiiiiiii," Puddin' screamed. He swatted the missile with his forearm. As hot water spilled on him he shook his clothes like there were bees in his shirt and pants. Widow Sanders, the conjure-woman, stood in a corner looking tense and evil.

"Get you," Tina yelled.

Puddin' leaped toward her and latched onto her shoulder. "Baby, you don't want to hurt your main man, do you?" Laughing, Puddin' dragged Tina to a chair and pushed her into it.

"Don't need you hanging 'round. We're hard-working folk," she said.

"Baby, I been waitin' so long. An' they told me I's gettin' out last month but the day come and I wan't let out . . . "

"Me and all my children's good hard-working folk. Don't need no shiftless convict hangin' 'round here."

"I guess I knows why. I hear you and Deacon Smith makes a

right sweet couple," Puddin' said with malevolence. "All of us common convicts knows about it . . . "

"Shut you nasty mouth. I got hard enough trouble keeping these children honest—least till they leave home—without you . . . "

"They ain't never goin' to 'mount to much. Dot too ugly or she'd have a boyfriend by now . . . "

Puddin' suddenly noticed that the children and a strange new face stared at him from the safety of the doorway.

Dorothy looked at her father, who she felt was lying but who couldn't be a liar, and tears ran unashamedly down her face already carved with sorrow as only a child's features can be effaced. Until she was dead she would never stop looking sadly after her father.

" . . . take Bocat," Puddin' continued unabated. "He's too stupid to do anything but pick cotton."

"Leave all my chillun alone, hear? I remember how it was before, you always cussing my chillun, scaring them half to death . . . "

"They are my children too. I do what I damn well please."

"Since you won't get gone, you might as well wash up. God willing, we going to eat soon and get on out to the field."

Widow Sanders shuffled about the kitchen in tired slippers, chattering to herself in the shack's steaming hot room where shiny quart bottles stuffed with tomatoes were lined on the sink and a large pot of tomatoes boiled on the stove next to a pot of sparkling empty jars and a kettle of sweet potatoes. "We been up all night canning," Widow Sanders said. "Now Tina's in a hurry to get finished and into the fields, this man come in here cuttin' the fool like he been around the rice pot," she muttered.

"What do you mean, I been around the rice pot?" Puddin' demanded.

"Somebody must've worked some roots on you son, maybe thrown some gooby dust in your path for you to be so mean to this here 'oman who ain't never been nothin' but good to ya."

"Roots, hell. The only root I got is right here," Puddin' said, grabbing at the crotch of his pants and taking hold of a handful of meat. "What you got there?" Puddin' asked, peeking into the kettle of yams. Before anyone could answer he grabbed the kettle and was walking out the door with it.

"You going to burn yourself," Tina called.

"No that devilman ain't," Widow Sanders said.

"Come back here with our dinner, man. I was going to candy them yams," Tina said.

In the yard Puddin' found Sam and Ethel, his two favorite hounds, poured the water off the yams and poured the hot sweets into their pan. The dogs jumped around him, smiling and wagging their tails. Burning their tongues on the potatoes, they nibbled carefully at the orange tubers with their front teeth. Puddin' could hear the women in the house cursing his name.

He looked over at the side of the house and saw the potato kiln intact. The mound of potatoes, protected from the weather by straw and dirt packed down, held plenty more of the sweet roots.

Full of a wondrous, luxurious satisfaction, Puddin' stripped to the waist and enjoyed laving his body with the silver-quick well water. The cold water stood beaded on his tight, black skin. Rises of keloidal scars ran in rows down Puddin's back as though a giant cat had scratched him. He shouted and spit water through sputtering lips and when water ran trickling down his back, he shook his butt like a roosting hen. From the corner of his eye he caught sight of Dot in the doorway of the house watching him while running her foot up and down the calf of her leg.

Entering the kitchen Puddin' heard Widow Sanders and Tina making over the stranger. If he wasn't dressed so poorly, Puddin' might have taken him to be a preacher.

"You're welcome to some breakfast," Widow Sanders said.

"He better not leave here without something in his stomach," Tina said while prodding a pot of grits with a spoon. On the counter were rows of freshly bottled and capped tomatoes.

Puddin' sat down at the kitchen table.

"Jesse, that there fool who just fed the 'taters I was cookin' for dinner to the dogs is my husband."

"How do, Mr. Moore," Jesse said, joining Puddin' at the table.

"Where you from?" Puddin' asked.

"Jackson."

Tina fried sizzling pieces of fatback in the skillet and then scrambled a heap of eggs in the grease. She pulled some cornbread from the oven and portioned out the vittles onto blue-trimmed earthenware.

"You live around these parts?" Puddin' asked.

"He's stayin' here," Tina said. "He's one of them freedom folks."

The word "freedom" caused Puddin's mouth to shut up like a steel trap and his eyes to frown at Tina.

"I don't know what you got to be so uppity about," Tina said. "He's an able-bodied man. We can use some real men around here. Nothin' but women and children left. Jesse, you feel free to stay here in the front room and I'll help you fix it up just like you want."

"Time was," Widow Sanders said, "thousands of folk lived here in Newtown. Once a cropper would farm and borrow a little for furnishings and seed. At the end o' the year the owner and the cropper split the cost and split the profit. But these days the owner shares the profit and takes the cost o' fertilizer, seed and such from the cropper's half."

"Last year I picked twenty-two bales and only made one hundred dollar. Why them bales must be worth fifteen hundred dollar," Tina said. "All we can do is the best we can. Work all day picking and all night canning and putting food up before the freeze. Slave fo' the boss . . . then slave fo' our-selves."

"Do you ever plant a little garden for yourselves?" Jesse asked.

"Sure 'nough. But ain't too many folk in 'Sippi who preserve. Them what did is forgettin'. Buyin' stuff in cans," Tina said.

"Some folk'll plant cotton right up to their front door. But a couple a folk around here grow corn, peas, squash, tomatoes and put it up," Widow Sanders said.

Tina slipped on her olive-green jacket and said, "I got to get out in the field. You comin' Jesse? Pud'?"

Jesse followed Tina to the door where they turned and looked back at Puddin' who still sat at the table wiping his plate with bread.

"I can work with you until noon," Jesse explained.

"I'm visiting my dear friend Anne this afternoon," Widow Sanders said.

"What about you?" Tina asked Puddin'.

"I got other things to do, 'oman."

"Tomorrow even Dot's goin' to be in the fields and Eliza-beth'll be takin' care of the babies. I sure ain't goin' to have you convict ass layin' up in my bed for *free*."

"Now Tina," Widow Sanders said. "Give him a day. And you oughtn't be so hard on the man. We never did find why he was arrested. He just walked out o' here one day and next thin' we knows he's in jail. I raised that man just like he was my own and I know him. He ain't evil, honey."

"He know why he was in there. Cause he's so big-headed. The newspaper say the Sheriff is lookin' for a Negro in a brown suit who stole some feed from Mr. Zakis. We all told Puddin' not to go out in his brown suit, but he had a hard head. He ought ta learn ta listen at someone who know somethin' some-time."

"Just leave me be, 'oman. I'll go tomorrow," Puddin' said. As Widow Sanders, Jesse and Tina walked out of the yard, Puddin'

went over to the corner behind the door and picked up his
shotgun and knew that the only place in the world he wanted
to be was deep in the swamps with his shotgun and his dogs.
On the top of the cupboard he found the shells.

Walking in the high fields, Sam and Ethel playfully bumped
up against Puddin'. He turned onto a road marked "Bridge
Out, Travel at Your Own Risk." Except for a few angry looking clouds the sky was clear as a glass of spring water. When he
came to the bridge, Puddin' automatically took a path leading
down into a clump of bushes beside the road where he found a
plank bridge that the pulpwood trucks used before the other
bridge was thought of. On the other side of the bridge was mud,
thick and tacky.

Great God, Puddin' thought, seeing a weather-worn one-
room building filled up with hay. They're storing hay in the old
schoolhouse. Puddin' was proud, but a bit sad, to see the fields
that he had cleared of stumps and rocks and seen bloom with
plants he'd cultivated, for those fields were grown wild. He saw
cows walking though the land that held the tumbled remains of
the church where he was married. Puddin' headed across a field
of broomstraw and, finally, into the wood. He avoided shallow
spots in the ground that he knew were wells hidden by over-
growth. He'd lost many a cow in those wells. Following a dry,
overgrown flood gulley, he made his way downhill through
thickening briars and bush toward the swamp. The autumn sun
penetrated the vine-covered trees that would have cloaked him
in a dim green light in the summer. His dogs fanned out, exploring different animal scents.

Puddin' heard the flow of water in the swamp before he saw
it, all slick-looking in the autumn noon sun; a sun that never
reached the zenith. He waded past trees covered with vines out
to a place where the water ran fast, knelt on a fallen log, placed
his parched lips on the sparkling water and sipped. The excited
barks of the dogs came cutting through the woods and he

moved toward the noise. Sam and Ethel had cornered a family of coons in a sweet gum tree. He raised his gun, aimed and banged down on them in one easy motion. The pump action seemed a part of his arm. In a very few seconds three coons lay bleeding on the ground.

Puddin' threw the game into his hunting bag and continued through the woods, sticking to the edge of the swamp. At first he didn't notice the darkening sky as his eyes searched the trees for squirrels or their nests, or coons and the holes they like to live in. He watched the hill sloping down to the water for signs of rabbit but it was as he'd feared when he'd seen how the land was running wild; varmints like mountain lions, wild hogs, hawks, and fox were killing off the rabbits, squirrels and other small critters. Finally darkness made him realize that a heavy storm was about to start and he looked for someplace to hide. He saw a patch of briars near a giant fallen tree but feared that wouldn't protect him if the storm turned out to be a tornado. Then he saw a place where the water had carved out a cave under the roots of a willow tree and climbed up in there with his dogs. He was afraid of snakes, but more afraid of the storm that finally came beating down upon the forest, cutting off the light and almost sucking the air from Puddin' with its force. The storm passed as quickly as it came and he continued his hunt as the sun sucked the water from the rot-covered ground and steam rose from the swamp.

As daylight seeped away through the trees, Puddin' found young trees with barked chewed off, indicating deer were tipping around. He didn't have time to look for them but the signs did give Puddin' the urge to return to the swamp as soon as he could.

Puddin' felt as though a weight had been lifted from his soul, but his freedom was an uneasy freedom, full of doubt. The warm soft weight in the bag on his back and the gun pressing down on his shoulder gave him a little comfort as he beat it through the woods toward home with his dogs trotting alertly beside him. With his free hand Puddin' cleared vines and briars from his path. By the time he reached the low fields the sun was resting like a tiny bird among the dark limbs of the trees behind him.

Puddin' quickened his step as he saw the lights of his house. Busting into the kitchen, he smiled at Tina's and Dot's startled faces. He set the gun in the corner and threw the bag from his shoulder.

"Lands but you near scared me to death," Tina said.

"What'd you catch, Daddy?" Dorothy asked.

Puddin' went into the bag and held two of the coons up by the tail. The duck lay wilted on the floor where it fell.

"Ha, I knows just what to do with them boys," Tina said. "You skin 'em . . . careful to take all the musk out . . . and I'll boil dem up wid some taters. That'll suck the gaminess out o' dem. Den we'll cook dem wid some candied sweets. Thank God you didn't give all the sweets to the dogs. We'll clean the duck and take it to Widow Sanders."

"Where'd you get them, Paw?" Dot asked.

"Well, I went on down around in de swamp and was drinking some water out in de stream when dem dogs sent up an awful noise and I know they done cornered some critter. Sho 'nough when I found dem boys they had dese here coons trapped up a tree and I banged down on one what was goin' for a hole in the tree and before he hit the gound I had banged down on anuder one. That last un was smart, though, and went aroun' t'ather side o' the tree. I just steps around a little and banged down on him too. I sure was hopin' fo' some rabbits though. They used to just jump up all around out dere and I'd allus come home wid a parcel o' dem."

Elizabeth, Pete and the baby stood in the doorway of the kitchen peeking at the coons. Behind them, reflecting through the hallway, was the noise and flashing blue-white light of the TV.

"Maybe we can fix a coonskin cap fo' them young uns," Puddin' said.

"They don' need no caps. You take them skins on down to the tanners and get that five dollars the nice white man's goin' ta give you," Tina fussed.

Suddenly everyone in the kitchen stopped and listened. Filtering through the night noises of crickets and the distant swamp sounds—sounds Widow Sanders called haints—was a noise in the back of the house. Tina ran to the door and grabbed the shotgun. "Who's there?" she shouted.

"Me."

"Put that gun down, 'oman," Puddin' said.

A tall angular fellow emerged from the kitchen doorway dressed in coveralls streaked with red and yellow mud.

"Hello, Paw," he said.

"Bocat," Puddin' shouted rising to slap the fellow on the shoulder. "Good to see ya, boy."

The girls nodded hello with awful respect and chanted in singsong voices, "Hello, brother Bo."

Bocat walked into the large bedroom just off the kitchen where he fell exhausted into a chair. Tina picked up a washbasin and box of soda and went into the bedroom. Puddin' followed her and watched from the door.

"Big bro' can't find no decent work," Tina explained to Puddin', at the same time admonishing Bocat, "he heps haul wood and does odd jobs. But say he won't work fo' no white man. Boy's a fool if'n you ask me. But I suppose the Lawd protect babes and fools."

Breaking into the conversation as he came down the hall from the front door Jesse said, "Remember your bible. For it is written, I will destroy the wisdom of the wise and will bring to nothing the understanding of the prudent."

Running into the room in a frill-covered blue dressing gown tied with a wide blue ribbon, Dorothy squeaked, "Jesse, you ought ta see what Daddy done caught." Elizabeth ran up to Jesse and pulled him into the kitchen.

Puddin' watched Tina help Bocat remove his boots and place his feet in a tub of warm solution of Epsom salts, then lie back in the soft chair with his coat and cap still uncomfortably upon his body.

"I waited around until all the union men were hired and finally got to work at the warehouse," Bocat said with a hopeless air. "At least I didn't go to the cotton fields."

Puddin' thought of the time years ago when he'd worked at the warehouse, the darkness of the trailers and trains where he sank his baling hook into box after box, pulling them onto his shoulder and flipping them onto a pallet until he'd fallen into a rhythm and didn't have to think as his body joined with the other sweating bodies slaving in the darkness. His body felt like an old outer garment, a crust that had little to do with the spark that was glowing deep inside. He walked into the kitchen and sat down while Dorothy fixed the coons and talked to the stranger.

"Ain't you scared," Dorothy said with her hungry black eyes brilliant.

"Scared of what?" Jesse asked.

"Scared of all the things goin' on and winter comin' . . . "

Jesse said nothing.

"No work in the winter," Elizabeth said.

"And no welfare checks this year for them who the whites don't like," Dorothy said. She shivered involuntarily and said, "Some people freezes up like icicles in the winter."

"Don't need no talk like that 'round here," Puddin' said. "You get your hind parts out of here dressed like dat. Some things right and some wrong. Won't have no daughter o' mine actin' like a hussy."

Dorothy howled and ran from the room. Elizabeth ran after her sister.

Puddin' leaned back in his chair, lighting a cigarette he'd taken from a pack on the table, comfortable in the company of the stranger. "It's getting cold," he said, wanting to know why Jesse was in town but not willing to get into another man's business. The acrid smell of wood burning in the stove mingled with the smell of the coons sharp in the air.

"You c'n stay in the front room tonight like you been doin'. But we don't need no roomer. Tomorrow we'll find you another place. Widow Sanders got room," Puddin' said.

"Don't no one know I stay here," Jesse said.

"Widow Sanders know. She better than the telephone. She know. That means everybody know," Puddin' said.

"Yes, sir," Jesse replied.

Soon the coons were boiled and baked with herbs and sweets and set on the table with the corn, greens and cornbread before Tina, Jesse, Puddin' and Bocat. The children ate standing near the table or sitting on the floor. "Well the Lord do provide, mysterious his wonders to behold," Widow Sanders said, coming in the door.

"Have a seat and get you some o' dis here coon and some o' dis corn Dorothy done got fo' us," Tina said.

"Land sakes, child, no," Widow Sanders said. "I et. Where'd you get them big coons from?"

"Puddin's shot 'em," Tina said.

"Well, I was on down around in de swamp . . . " Puddin' said.

"Hush you. Let's bless dis here food afore it get cold so's we c'n start eatin'," Tina said.

"I was just goin' ta . . . " Puddin' said.

"Bless the food, man," Tina demanded.

Puddin' thought for a while. In the brief silence the ten o'clock train whistle blew forcing upon everyone at the table the frightening recognition that another day had passed. Puddin' noticed that Bocat didn't bow his head and was troubled.

"Dear Lord make us truly thankful for the food we are about to receive for the nourishment of our body for Christ's sake, amen."

"Amen," everyone said except Bocat.

"Don't you believe in prayer, boy?" Puddin' asked Bocat.

Bocat looked into the faces of the people around the table. Jesse looked down into his plate. "Tell us about the hunt," he said.

And Puddin', frightened by what his son might say, once again told the story of how he banged down on them critters in the swamp.

When the razor-sharp shrill sound of the twelve o'clock train was raised in the night, Puddin' lay in his bed next to Tina. Bocat was on a cot nearby and Puddin' could sense that he was not asleep. From the girls' room came the sound of brass and horns playing "America the Beautiful" as the TV closed down for the night. Out in the living room Jesse slept on the couch next to a mattress thrown on the floor for the babies who'd been evicted from Tina's bed.

"Baby, baby, baby," he whispered in the black velvet night, rocking her slowly in his arms until their bodies found one another and he marveled at her strength and shouted praises to her soft receptiveness.

V

16

Saturday in Camp Grove

PUDDIN' SAT ON THE EDGE of his bed in the patchwork light
of the window. His body was void of energy; it seemed to belong
to someone else. Finally summoning his senses he felt he'd risen
from beneath a blanket of cool earth. This was the day he'd
search for work, for he'd not live off Tina and become a burden
to the family.

Peering from the window beside the bed he shivered at the
sight of the cold morning sun. Tina and Pete and Baby Brother
were scrambled together amid the tangled bedclothes. Early in
the morning the babies had cried out for their mother and

refused to sleep in the front room. Bocat lay twisted in troubled sleep on the cot in the corner of the room. He looked into the next room and saw Dot stretched across her bed. The girl was fast becoming a woman and would soon be leaving home to go off with some smooth-faced boy.

Puddin' looked at the yellowing newspaper society pages pasted over his head with flour and water and the comic pages on the opposite wall and was angered to see several new additions. The children had pasted the news section in his room where he'd always strictly directed them to paste nothing but the society section for Tina and the comics for him.

There was no time to wait. Now he had to act. When he'd been arrested a year before and charged with thievery he'd waited for Miss Elizabeth Fletcher to bail him out. He'd kept her grass, shrubs, horses and dogs in prize-winning shape. But Miss Elizabeth never turned up. He waited for a month and then was tried in two minutes. None of his friends were in court. In jail he'd waited to be released on good behavior, but had served more than his time. In jail he met men like Gabriel who'd killed his wife and was given six months. Puddin' was thoroughly confused by the consequence of the law.

Puddin' shook Bocat awake. "Time for work," he whispered.

They dressed silently and then Puddin' dug around in the tool shed and found his old lunch pail. He cleaned it with a rag and put a sandwich in it he'd made with a piece of ham he'd fished out of the pot of greens—their last piece of meat. All the coon was gone. He snatched up the pail and slipped out the back door with Bocat. A musk smell from the garbage pile near the back gate was sharpened by morning dampness.

Puddles on the morning lanes and streets. Light shining upon them like silver coins. The land seemed to bleed, the rising sun staining the eastern horizon red. In the lingering night, Puddin's squeaking lunch pail commented upon the quiet dawning. The two men scurried silently through the streets of a white neighborhood bordering the business district, awkward giants trespassing a mysterious fairy-tale city.

Garbage cans were set neatly in front of the white-columned grand old houses. Scrounging through the garbage was an old lady. Before she turned her gray face from Puddin' and took to filling the carpetbag that hung over her shoulder with scraps, he recognized Mrs. Gittens and was ashamed to call her name.

Near the river silhouettes of cranes, chimneys and water towers etched the sky. The streets were empty except for a gang of men around a fire roughly contained in an oil drum. "There's J. V.," Bocat said and waved. One of the men around the oil drum waved back. On the highway above the docks the morning rush of cars into Matchez had started.

"Hear they needs a lot of hep at Nicholson's warehouse," Bocat said. "Me, I'm workin' down on dock three in warehouse eighty." Bocat waved good-bye to Puddin' as the metal steps of warehouse 260 clanged under the tread of Puddin's brogans.

Corrugated metal siding carefully preserved the cool damp of the night. A gang of workers, sipping hot coffee, stared suspiciously at Puddin'.

"Any work today?" he asked.

"Ask the boss," one said. " . . . be in around ten."

Puddin' sat on a packing crate. He'd wait. He looked at his hands. The joints were swollen from working in wet and cold. Black, tight, leathery skin emphasized the veins. Between the bones of his hands bulged knotty muscles. Smooth scar tissues covered much of his hands. It had come from the scalding food and pots and plates he'd handled in the prison kitchen.

"You want to see me, boy?" a deep barrel-chested, red-necked fellow asked.

" . . . lookin' fo' a job, boss," Puddin' said.

"You got a card?" the boss growled through a ragged-slash mouth.

"A card?"

"A paid-up union card."

"No, suh."

"Then you got to wait until we sure we hired all the union men what wants work today."

Puddin' looked the man straight in the eye. "But Mr. Nicholson say I could have a job . . . "

"Nicholson's up in the front office. If he say you got a job, then you got a job. The union'll get down on us but . . . "

Puddin' walked through aisles of crates whose surfaces were drenched with manila sunlight slanting in from the skylight to the office. He walked quietly into the office and softly asked the secretary if he could see Nicholson.

Greatly evidencing her discomfort, the secretary went into an inner office as all the typists and clerks stopped work to stare at Puddin'. The secretary reentered the main office with Bernard Nicholson following her.

"What is it?" Nicholson snapped.

"Couple o' years ago, I's doin' some common labor fo' your paw and he say any time I needed a job to come down to your warehouse. I sure needs a job now, Mr. Nicholson, sir." Puddin' lied because he felt that neither the white man nor his father would remember whether a common nigger like himself had ever done common labor for him two years ago.

"Oh yes," Bernard said good-naturedly. "Let me call Paw, he'd be glad to hear you stopped by."

Puddin' felt trapped. He hadn't counted on this.

Bernard picked up the phone and dialed.

"Hello, Paw. Yes. Fellow down here says he worked for you a couple of years ago. Nat Moore. Wants a job. Says you told him he could count on us . . . I just wanted to know . . . what?" Bernard placed the phone down and his voice changed to a deadly seriousness as he said, "You ain't the Nat what's married to Tina Moore? The fellow they call Puddin' over at the jailhouse?"

"Yes suh."

"We don't hire convicts," Bernard said.

"Yes suh," Puddin' said, turning to go.

"But if you go out to the farm you can get some work pick-ing," Bernard said, softening his voice in a benevolent gesture.

"But that's what I did in jail. Pick cotton on your farm. I thought . . . "

"You think pickin' cotton's too dirty?" Bernard said, his voice growing deeper and menacing. "And who the hell asked you to think?" Bernard laughed. The clerks and secretaries saw Nicholson laugh and they all started laughing.

Violent anger rose to a peak within Puddin' but was quickly turned inward. He felt it hot in the pit of his stomach. Then the anger turned into fear of the attack he couldn't answer.

"Go tell your leader, Jacob Blue, you need a job," Nicholson called after him as he hurried through the warehouse past aisles of boxes. The black workers looked at Puddin' with fright as though expecting him to be shot down any moment. Outside in the morning sun, Puddin' stopped running and slowly headed back to Newtown.

Puddin' went to the Hansen lumberyard by the tracks, he humbly approached Horvitz and Zakis Green Dot Grocery and hung around Brown's gas station. But he found no one inter-ested in hiring him. About the time his feet decided they were too tired to carry him any more, he went on down to Fats's and bought a thirty-five-cent pint. He counted the money out of the five dollars he'd managed to pull together in jail selling fermented juices, mashes and extracts from the kitchen.

He drank his wine and ate lunch while watching the heavy Saturday afternoon action. The noise of the weekend street was cut off in the poolroom where there hung a lifeless silence. There was a deathly quiet as Fats lined up a shot. Fats lowered his face to the same level as the table and placed the stick in a postion to slice the ball to bank left and come back up the table after hitting at least two balls toward their pockets. It was said around the pool hall that when you played with Fats you would lose the game if you lost the toss of the coin for the first shot. After Fats poked the cue ball a deft stroke he reflectively watched the balls play the roles he'd assigned them. The first ball the cue ball hit jumped into the pocket, the second ball was knocked closer to the pocket and the cue moved back up the table for an easy set-up. The shiny multicolored balls that moved about with mathematical precision grouping and regrouping according to the laws of pool-ball behavior had a mystical air of predestination about them. Some believed the low balls were lucky because the seven was low and some believed the lows would win because thirteen was a high ball. Among the rows of sticks hanging on the walls were long sticks that everyone knew were custom-made and reserved for two men from Jackson who, regularly as clockwork, came to Matchez on weekends adding a touch of professionalism to the game, taking on all bettors and running the stakes up in the hundreds of dollars. No one paid Puddin' any mind for he'd never regularly visited such places before his arrest but Puddin' felt everyone in the place surely knew that he was just come from the chain gang. His well-muscled body, short-barbered hair, his walk and the way he looked men in the face surely gave him away. Everyone knew, he thought, and moved uneasily from the pool hall. He felt everyone's eyes glued to his back. He tried to straighten up and walk with longer strides among the usual Saturday street crowds.

Sweating, heavy eyelids over burning eyes, lips feeling thick, Puddin' floated up to the edge of a crowd of black folk listening to a speaker on the corner of Pearl and Mangrum.

"Come to the church tonight at eight and hear Dr. Jacob Blue tells us what we got to do to get better jobs, education, health . . . " Puddin' had heard rumors of Jacob's candidacy in jail but found it hard to believe that the fat prosperous doctor whom he'd played with when they were young and hungry children was doing such a fool thing. When the police roared up in a patrol car, Puddin' inconspicuously parted from the crowd and disappeared into an alley.

Turning the corner at the end of the alley, Puddin' found a bunch of men shooting craps near a whiskey fire. He nodded to the others and stood around warming himself and sharing butts with fellows hoping that someone would pull out the whiskey bottle he knew they were hiding somewhere in the group. One fellow was short with a large head that had one eye missing. Another high-yellow fellow who took after a Mexican kept playing the fool. "Come on, baby, work for me," he told the dice when his turn came. A third fellow seemed to be a worker for he was dressed in brogans, work pants and hooded sweatshirt. Soon High Yellow had pulled in all the pennies.

"You sure are lucky," the worker said.

"Sho 'nough," he said. "Let's drink to my luck. You too fella," he called to Puddin'. They all marched back along Pearl Street to Fats's and through the pool hall into the back-room bar and dancehall.

"A pint fo' each o' my friends."

Puddin' accepted the wine and greedily gulped it down.

"This here yaller motherfucker got more luck than a rabbit," the big fellow said.

As he was about to put his bottle to his lips the mulatto spit a pair of dice from his mouth and held them for everyone to see; they were full of sixes and ones. He laughed, "You boys didn't have no win."

The big fellow slapped him across the face and a few more dice sprang out—or perhaps teeth. Then he whipped out a razor and slit the fellow's throat from ear to ear. High Yellow's body dropped heavily to the floor where blood gushed from it like a stuck pig. In his eyes was the fright of a man who knew he was dead. Puddin' didn't think the law would worry much about one more dead nigger or even a Mexican, but he wasn't for taking chances and fled through the back door. As he passed people on his way out, no one seemed excited or even to care much. A few curious people went over to stare at the man's wound. Suddenly sobered, Puddin' headed for home. He used all the shortcuts he could, but was careful not to run or even appear in a hurry because nothing was more suspicious than a nigger running. When you were in a hurry it was best to go slow and when you had nothing to do, it was always best to appear in a hurry.

As Puddin' neared home he noticed the eyes of the neighbors staring at him. Even Widow Sanders peeked from a crack to curse them all.

Then he saw, large as the hand of death, a white paper tacked on his door, marking his house from among the houses in the row as having received the attention of the Sheriff's office. Puddin' couldn't read the notice, but tore it from his door and went trembling to the kitchen where he sat at the table staring at the paper. If only he could read it he could do something to try and ward the evil from his house. But he would have to wait until Tina and the children returned.

17

Piss in the Cotton

"ALL RIGHT GIRL, GET UP," Tina told Dot, standing over
her bed. Dot had stayed in school longer than any of her friends
or brother and hadn't been forced to go into the field but now
she would have to work along with the women and children
picking cotton because of the desperate need of her family for
money.

"You ain't done nothin' but get in trouble staying at home.
Stealin' dat corn was the last straw. Dat school ain't teachin'
you nothin'. When I's your age I's pickin' as much as a lot o'
men," Tina said.

Dot dressed in the new work clothes Tina had bought her Friday, careful to fill her bra with socks in order to show the other girls that she was progressing as fast as they toward what everyone called "the miracle that's happening in your body." When all of the girls stood around comparing the sizes of their breasts she had nothing to show and had been driven one day to fondle her little boobies until they got sore and had swollen.

Pete, Baby Bro', Elizabeth and Jesse were at the table when Dot climbed in her chair. Peaceful seconds followed while Tina blessed the food. God was watching over all. Dot dreamed of church. Hot sweating bodies bouncing. Fat women fainting. The music that made her cry and pat her feet. Outside the church in the shade of trees, tables burdened with food, soda and pink lemonade. In the church the preacher shouting "Save us Jesus. Jesus is in the church, hump. Jesus takes many forms, hump. Jesus can Reeeeelieve you of yur sufferin's, hump." As the black bespectacled deacon shouted, "Yes Lawd," a sister started to sing, "Were you there when they crucified ma lawd? Wur yu there when they . . . "

"Pass yo plate," Tina told Dot.

"I'm not hungry," she whispered.

"Listen, you better be real hungry. We worked hard to get dis food. And you got a lot o' work to do." Tina took the plate and piled it up high with eggs and grits.

Dot found it physically impossible to stuff one morsel of food past the nervous knot that formed in her throat. Viciously attacking her plate of food, Tina sent munching noises from her end of the table. Suddenly Elizabeth kicked Dot about some old grudge they'd had Friday she could barely remember. Dot kicked the little devil back and stole a biscuit from her plate.

"You children stop that now," Tina said.

"Ma," Dot said.

"What."

"You ain't never picked wet cotton afore," Dot said, remembering the heavy, but brief, Friday rain.

"If'n I thought we wasn't goin' ta work, I'd be done started cannin' or washin' and ironin'," Tina replied.

"The sun's goin' ta be pretty hot today," Jesse said, looking out the kitchen window.

"That's right," Tina said.

Before they left the house, Dot decided in order not to disgrace herself, she would stay right up with the older women and do whatever they did as fast as they did it. Tina gave some instructions to Elizabeth about how to care for Pete and Baby Bro' and they left the warm house.

Outside the damp dirt smelled like the earth in the neighborhood she'd visited several times with her paw. He'd carried a brown-paper bundle in one hand and held onto her with the other. Green plants covered the ground in the neighborhood of large houses and monstrous lawns. Puddin' would change his clothes and cut the grass, pull up weeds in flower beds and throw trash into a wire basket where flames danced about and paper turned into smoke. An old white lady called Miss Ethel once gave Dot a couple of pennies and she had said to the pretty lady exactly what Puddin' told her to, "Thank you, mam," and the old lady, who seemed to be constantly sad, smiled.

They raced the sun, rising full of hope, to the field. The warmth of the grits, gravy and egg breakfast in Dot's stomach helped her face the chill of the morning. Huddles of men, women and children broke up when the tall dark trucks pulled into the road and everyone climbed into the backs of trucks, boots making loud, hollow noises on the metal truck floor. Wind sweeping past Dot's face as she leaned over the rail of the truck watered her eyes and blurred the lush green along Route 49. Jesse stood in the crowded truck talking to the men around him. "Tonight at Mount Moriah Baptist Church," Dot heard him say.

"Lot of trouble," an old man mumbled.

"Votin's white folk's business," another fellow said.

"You think there'll be work?" Tina asked, unsure of herself.

"It were dry 'nough afore the sun set yesterday," the old man affirmed. "But it still ain't dried the ground good enough fo' the machines."

Coming over the hills near Yazoo City they came upon the Delta—a low flat expanse of cultivated alluvium. Riding high up on tractors in the fields were tractor drivers tending a third planting.

"Them sons-a-bitches think they big shit," the old man said.

"They make four buck a day and think they ain't cullud," Tina said.

"Shit," a young fellow laughed and spat over the side of the truck. He watched the spittle hang in the air parallel to the truck and then arc toward the road.

On the other side of the road the highway hummed with the wheels of log trucks and cotton trucks pushing toward Matchez. In the November fields where the truck stopped, flowers and grass waited upon winter's anesthetizing blow. Closed flowers and plants gone to seed reminded Dot of the death and cold the season promised. Dot picked a sack from a pile and followed a girl to the end of a row and began picking next to her copying her every move. Soon an ache settled in her back and fingers as the picking and dragging the sack became automatic and sweat flowed evenly over her heavily clothed body. The sun played a trick on Dot and hung in the sky like a clock pendulum at the peak of its swing, unmoving.

Ants crawled through the sweet smelling green weeds around the cotton plants. Rough men snatched at the white blossoms. Brown men picked and crawled, sweating in the sun. The hot fire in the sky hurt her eyes. Dot wanted to run to the well and stand in the shade of a tree and drink the cool, metallic-tasting well water, but there was neither shade nor water; there was only the sun, burning, burning.

Feeling the urge to urinate, Dot asked the girl in the next row where the outhouse was located. "Piss in the cotton," the girl said, lowering her panties and squatting over her sack of cotton and letting go a powerful stream of urine. Dot copied her. After she'd finished the big girl explained, "When yo' picks fo' the white man yo' puts sticks and stones in it and pisses." Dot was learning. She wondered if the big girl noticed that the lumps on her breasts under her coat were larger today.

At the end of the day when the sun swung quickly toward the horizon Dot was crawling stiffly. The strap of the sack cut into her shoulder and her side was sore where the trailing bag of cotton hit each time she moved. The older girl was nowhere in sight but she didn't care.

"We can go," Tina said, startling her.

Without a word Dorothy followed Tina back to the truck. Two of the strongest men in the group got under the yoke of the scale and grunted as they stood. As the cotton was weighed the tally man kept his hand on the cotton. Thus Dot saw that while you might cheat the man out of ten dollars he cheated you out of hundreds.

"Where's Jesse?" Dot asked.

"He left about noon," Tina said. "Some fellas in a truck come an' picked him up."

Sundown brought movement of trucks packed with workers and silent huddles of people moving along the road heading to their stingy meals, movement of children running from the goblin-filled night to parents' homes, of well-fed people racing along the highway in big cars, of lone men in thick coats and tweed caps walking along the road smoking pipes like little chimneys.

Often during the summers Dot had taken trips North with her family to pick potatoes in New Jersey. Despite the aching work and ugly work camps, she loved the trip, making a few pennies for her own pocket as well as helping the family, going into the big New Jersey towns for a soda at a fountain where you could sit next to white folk and not be spat upon and then the wonderful ride in her father's old car to the water, the wonderful ferry ride across what she thought must have been the Atlantic Ocean to Paris, France, to watch the Dodgers and Yankees play baseball. The cotton field was nothing but another way of slaving.

When Dot returned home she found Puddin' seated at the kitchen table sadly staring at a piece of paper. She raced to the bathroom to be the first to get in the tub. After everyone else had bathed the water would be cold. The hard shiny bathroom smelled of wetness. Steam rose from a smooth enamel tub. She scrubbed with a rough cloth. She scrubbed under the arms, behind the ears, the toes. The slippery soap smelled like bright yellow flowers with fat bumblebees dancing about them. The sleepy hot water and her slippery fingers caressed her body. The ceiling lights looked fuzzy through the hazy mirror. The swishing water raised mountains of foam. She raked the skin from her body with a monstrous towel. The wet linoleum floor froze her feet. The last drops of water rushed noisily down the drain. She stepped into warm-smelling pajamas and gathered up her clothes filthy with red and yellow mud. She got on her knees and scrubbed the tub and then started the water for the next person.

It was when she came from the bathroom, sweet-smelling, limber, the pains of the day forgotten, that she realized something terrible had happened. Tina sat at the kitchen table crying. Puddin', Elizabeth and even Pete stared at the piece of paper.

Dorothy read the paper. "You are hereby ordered to vacate the premises by the order of the City Court of Matchez." It was signed by Judge Clayton. It also said "Served by Sheriff Tate."

"It's cause o' that freedom rider," Puddin' said.

"We been here in Camp Grove fo' so long," Tina cried. "We pay our rent. Sometimes it a little late but we pay."

"Soon as Bo come we goin' to get the hell out o' here."

"Where we goin'?" Tina asked. "Notice say we don't have ta go till Monday."

"You just get yourse'f ready, 'oman."

"We got to clean the place up too. I ain't never left a place so the next folk would ask what kind o' housekeeper I be."

"Don't you worry your head none 'oman. Pack up. We's movin' on."

"Where we goin' Pa?" Dot asked.

"Jackson, Memphis, Chi'. What do it matter long as we goin' way from here?" Puddin' said.

"How we travelin'? Walkin'?" Tina asked sarcastically.

"Don't you worry yourse'f none." Puddin' took his shotgun from the corner and walked out the kitchen door. Tina ran up to him and grabbed his arm, "What you goin' ta do, man?" she screamed. Puddin' shrugged her hand off and left. Outside in the dark they heard the dogs bark. Tina cried as she got together her things, trying to decide what should stay and what to take.

When Bocat came home from work looking as though he were about to draw his last breath, Tina seemed afraid to tell him. She let him read the notice for himself. "The sons-o-bitches," he said, falling into a kitchen chair.

"When your pa found out what the notice say he took out o' here with his gun and dogs," Tina said.

Bocat's eyes hardened with fear. "He say where he goin'?" he asked, breathing deep.

"Not a word," Tina said.

The noise of a car backfiring in the distance startled everyone in the kitchen. They listened quietly as the car approached. Bocat ran to the front window. The car stopped in front of the house and the headlights were turned out. Someone got out and walked toward the house. Bocat went to the door and called out, "Who dat?"

"Me."

"It's Pa," Bocat shouted.

Standing before the questioning eyes of his family Puddin' explained, "I sold ma gun and dogs and got dis here car from the Turners. Let's get packed."

"Let's have one last meal and spend one last night here," Tina suggested.

"Let's get packed first," Puddin' said. "Maybe."

"I come as soon as I heard," Jesse said coming through the front door and down the hall. "Everyone else in Camp Grove got the same notice."

"How d'ya know?" Tina asked.

"Widow Sanders told me and then I visited everyone. Everyone ought to come to the meeting tonight. Let's talk about this over at the church."

Dot agreed with Jesse and looked at her mother and brother. They seemed for it. But Puddin' said, "What good is talkin' about votin' and freedom goin' ta do us?"

"Maybe there's something we can do about the evictions as a group. You know why you got to move, don't ya?"

"Yeah, the Sheriff say so," Tina said.

"No, it's cause there's goin' ta be urban renewal. They're goin' ta build projects here in Camp Grove."

"Is that so? Told ya that boy was smart," Tina said.

"There's laws. Like they supposed to see you can find another house before they kick you out. And they're supposed to help pay for movin' . . ."

"Well, I don't guess it can't hurt none just to see what they sayin'," Puddin' admitted.

Dot dressed in blue jeans and sweatshirt and started packing. When Tina sent her around the neighborhood looking for boxes she saw that everyone else was busy at the same thing. She was frightened as once more in her life an unseen force was causing great turmoil. When they'd packed the cups, saucers, plates, ash trays, silverware, toilet articles and clothes, they all piled into the old car Puddin' had bought and headed toward the meeting.

VI

IV

18

How Bernard Spent Friday
and Saturday

BERNARD STUDIED THE CROWD of newsmen standing about
the office. Over the years he'd come to know them well and
trusted none of them to tell more than half-truths. They were
the only men he knew who could contradict themselves within
one sentence. Kuetman of AX News had rushed in from Jackson
for the noon conference and he had to hurry if he was going to
make the morning papers. Kuetman was there for the usual

reasons—he was sent to do a job on Sheriff Tate for the Northern Liberal press and he would, through subtle innuendo as well
as outright lies, attack everyone it might profit him to attack.

Fat Al Lowman, the stolid journalist from the *Atlantic Patriot*,
was the only one of the reporters who looked the part of a
newspaperman with his London Fog and broad-brimmed hat
jerked down to one side of his placid face. The other stringers
for various papers and newsservices looked like young men on
their way up and were properly dressed in sharkskin Madison
Avenue suits, tight-fitting, short-cut, and sissified.

Then there were the technicians; the cameramen with the big
black bags full of instruments. Bernard could sympathize with
them for they were a breed of men who cared neither for the
subjects they were filming or recording nor for the bull sessions
in bars that took place after a job where the newsmen gossiped
about all the things not fit to print. The technicians rarely knew
what subject they were filming, they just cared about voice level
and reading light meters. Slander could be left to the editors as
far as they were concerned.

"Damn hot," Bernard said.

"Ain't the heat so much as the humidity. It's the river what
does it," Lowman said.

"I think it's goin' a rain," Tate said.

"Sheriff, you write up a press release?" Kuetner wanted to
know. "If you could just give me a statement, I could get back
to Jackson. The Sox are playing the Tigers tonight."

Lowman and Kuetner whispered to one another, rolling their
eyes at John Frailty. Bernard was amused that the presence of
Frailty caused so much speculation among the reporters.
And it was all due to Machiavelli, who advised princes interested in keeping power to engage in public displays of gener-
osity on the one hand while being ruthlessly brutal to enemies
on the other?

Tate sat down and motioned for John to sit on one side of
him. Tate looked extremely uncomfortable in his brown shirt

and tight tie. He constantly punched his pudgy finger under his collar.

Bernard lit a long green cigar—Cuban—and leaned against the wall near the window. On that day Bernard had taken advantage of his title as deputy sheriff to don two pearl-handled nickel-plated horse pistols, or magnums.

The cameramen flashed on electric floodlights and the faces of Tate and Frailty began to gleam. As perspiration rolled from Tate's face he wiped himself with a pastel-shaded silk handkerchief.

"Ready?" an impatient voice asked.

"If you boys is ready, I'll give you my statement," Tate said. "I called this here press conference to announce that John Frailty, the nigger sitting right here beside me now, has been appointed a deputy sheriff."

Kuetner had to stifle a laugh.

Bernard thought maybe Lowman was right in constantly insisting that the Northern press should be excluded from conferences that would have broad effect on the South and that were politically delicate.

"Why'd you appoint John?" Burnside of the *Matchez Chronicle* asked. "Aren't there other qualified men?"

"Frailty ain't really doing me any favors. The nigra is sacrificing himself because he got money from his own business and can afford to be deputy. Nothin' unusual about me appointin' a responsible citizen deputy. Nearly every white man in this town is already a deputy . . ."

"Are you a racial moderate?" Kuetman asked.

"The federal government is forcin' me to become a moderate," Tate said.

"Is John qualified?" Burnside asked.

"He's a good Matchez boy. I've had dealings with him and his paw at different times. I've found that he's an average colored fellow with average intelligence. If he's willing to serve as my deputy, that's his perogative."

"Is this related to your campaign for reelection or the campaign of Whiteman, whose slate you're on?" Lowman asked.

"Now I ain't sayin' that dis here has anything whatsoever to do with politics. That's all, gentlemen," Tate said.

"Do you think Jacob Blue has a chance?" Kuetman asked.

"No comment."

"Will you block the move of Negroes to have a mass meeting tomorrow afternoon?"

Tate's mouth dropped open in surprise. "I didn't know they planned one."

"They got leaflets all over town! "

"As long as they obey the law, I can't do nothin'," Tate said.

"We believe in freedom of assembly," Bernard said.

While the technicians dismantled the equipment, the reporters used the courthouse phones to call stories to their desks. Burnside and Lowman came to Bernard and joked, "You fellows surprised everyone with this move." "You have any comment, Bernard?" Burnside asked.

"This appointment proves that there is no prejudice among the good Democrats of this town," he said.

"Thank you," they said and, grinning like lap dogs, walked away writing on their pads.

Shaking hands and patting backs, Bernard saw the newsmen from the room. "Now let's get down to business. We need some people from your section of town to drive voters to the polls and to poll watch," he told Frailty.

"Best way to do that is to fill folks' cars up wid gas," Tate said.

Bernard finished his business with Tate and Frailty, stopped at the Tax Assessor's office to check the title of a parcel of land he was interested in and then left the courthouse. Outside the air and streets had been washed clean by a quick shower.

Far off down the street he saw a Negro walking alone, across the street was a road gang of convicts and a troop of boy scouts were climbing all over the courthouse. In the municipal parking lot Bernard placed his pistols in the trunk of his car and headed up Main Street toward Hofstra Training School.

He stopped in the school's drive and beeped his horn, expecting to see her run to the car, her red hair streaming behind her in a pony tail. While he waited he thought he'd have a drink and pressed a button on the dash opening the glove compartment revealing a bar stocked with miniature bottles of liquor. He loved to buy cars with little extras built in and was on the lookout for a James Bond car. He mixed a drink and waited. He could see the Mississippi slowly twisting through the land, its white beaches ablaze in the sunlight, its lazy muddy water not giving the least hint of its power. The old river was resting up for later in the year when it would change direction flooding a lot of land and cutting new channels.

The front door opened and Sally Turner Reeves stuck her head out. She waved and he jumped out of the car. As he approached the front door he noticed that Sally was crying. "Laura wants to see you in her room," she squeaked and ran away crying.

He ran upstairs and hunted among the rows of rooms for Laura's. Several girls he ran into were shocked to see him at first but smiled or giggled when they recognized him.

Bernard finally bumped into Ethel Wisner coming out of a room. "Laura's in there aborting your child. We found this," she said, holding up a bottle for Bernard to read the label. It said "Quinine."

"But that's impossible."

"We called Doc Tyson and he came over and gave her some shots to prevent infection and ease her nerves. I've tried so hard to bring Laura up properly. It'll just kill her uncle."

"I don't think the child's mine and even if it is I wouldn't have wanted her to do this."

"I've seen you two sneaking off to be alone," Ethel said with loathing.

"Listen, honey, don't act so righteous to me. Your only claim to fame is that you once shacked up during the war with Ron Sterling, the Nation's Leading Poet."

"It was a liaison. I was young."

"Liaison, hell. You were his whore. And something you never tell anyone is that you left him when the government arrested him for his belief in facism. That would go over big among our friends," Bernard said vindictively. He left Ethel in the hall and burst on into the room.

Laura was sprawled across the bed dressed only in a house smock. She was moaning low from a face red with crying. Her outstretched hands opened and closed, grasping at air. Suddenly she doubled up and moaned louder. "Go away," she said when she saw him.

"Why did you kill my child?" Bernard demanded.

"Go away. Go away," she murmured.

"Anyway you said your menses were almost starting. How could this happen?"

Laura ran to the bathroom and he heard liquid sounds from there.

"Is there anything I can do?"

"No," she groaned.

Bernard saw an unopened bottle of champagne on Laura's dresser she'd been given months before on her birthday and ripped the tinfoil and wire mesh from the top. Popping off with a bang, the top hit the ceiling. Laura stuck her head from the bathroom door.

"Just opening some champagne," Bernard said, lifting the bottle to his lips.

Laura came exhausted and wet with perspiration from the bathroom and fell onto the bed.

"What's wrong?" Bernard asked.

"I just pissed out one pound of meat," she cried and buried her head in her arms, sobbing heavily. "I thought this would be easier than the birth pain, the nausea, the muscle spasms, the incision, purging the afterbirth, the uncomfortable stitches like I saw on Rosa Gilsby. But I was wrong. But you don't have to worry about none of this shit."

"I would have married you, Laura. Now we're disgraced."

"The only people who know are Ethel, Doc Tyson and my roommate, Sally. This kind of secret is shared by many girls in this place. More than you think. Nobody would tell."

"Everyone knows. How many months were you gone?" Bernard asked.

"Two."

"But honey, we only been at it for a little over a month."

"Well, a month and a half. I don't know. What's the difference."

"I can find out from Doc Tyson. Maybe that little bugger you just finished flushing into the Mississippi wasn't mine."

"You are an evil man," she said, staring at him with her emerald-like black eyes. "Who else in this town would I let touch me? Sol Lorchman? Ephram's son? A Jew? Lenny Hansen, whose people were cutting down trees when my folks were sitting in Congress? Teddy Zakis, whose parents have got a nice Greek girl hand-picked for him? Please don't leave, Bernie."

"I got some business."

"One reason I did it, I guess, is cause o' my figure," she said.

"I wouldn't find nothin' wrong with your shape, never."

"But they say I'll make a good model."

"They? Model?"

"Herr Schneider says he'll get me in with United Modeling Agency in New York. He says I got a perfect shape for modeling."

"But why do you want to work?"

"It'll give me a chance to see New York again. And I could study actin'. Besides, it pays fifty dollars an hour. You could fly up every weekend or I could fly down."

"So, Schneider put these stupid ideas in your head. Judge Clayton warned me."

"Bernie."

"Yes?"

"I luv you."

Admonishing her to get some rest, he kissed Laura good-bye and went down to his car. He took the guns from the trunk and strapped them on again.

Bernard hoped and prayed that Laura was right and that the word wouldn't spread quickly around the town about her peculiar problem the name of which he could only think of with the greatest distaste—abortion. If such gossip flew it would place a sticky social barrier in his path. He knew that if he worked diligently at his political affairs, the ultimate result of the turmoil in the town, stirred up by a few Negroes and the federal government, would be the strengthening of his and his friends' control in town affairs.

Turning left from Main onto Magnolia, Bernard drove past St. Puce's and turned into the drive of the Piedmont Center City Club. It had the design of a palace he'd once seen in Paris and was very similar to the executive building once used by the Secretary of State near the White House in Washington. The building's exterior was marked by ornate woodwork, no doubt the handiwork of antebellum slaves, and its interior was marked by the ostentatious show of wealth one could expect in the club of the new rich of the area. Bernard, of course, belonged to the exclusive Alexander Club, but found the Piedmont Club a convenient place near downtown to meet friends.

"Your party's in the Teak Room, sir," Ned told Bernard.

"Is Fannie here? I don't want anyone but Fannie," Bernard said. Old Ned smiled and nodded his head. Bernard checked the guest book. Janice and Ephram Lorchman had signed, for although he had sponsored them as members a year before, their application had not yet been considered by the board. Art

Reid had signed as an out-of-town guest and farther down the list he found the name of Al Mizel written in barely legible scrawl. The he took the elevator up three flights to the Teak Room.

Along with Janice, Ephram, Art and Al he found Terressa McCloud Beufort III. While exchanging greetings Janice asked if Laura would be along and he had the uncomfortable feeling that she knew. Surprising everyone, Sam Nicholson came in upon Bernard's heels.

"I was dining downtown and Ben told me you were up here. Do you mind if I join you?" he said to his son and guests.

Bernard pulled a chair out for his father at the head of the table.

"Bernard," said Janice Lorchman, whom he had interrupted in the middle of one of her typical big ideas by his abrupt entrance, "perhaps you or your father can help us. Terressa and I were just arguing over whether or not man comes into the world as Leibniz says, already equipped with full human status, or do you agree with Terressa and her Lockean theory that man is a *tabula rasa* at birth. You see we're taking a course at Old Miss and . . ."

"Have you ordered?" Bernard interrupted. "Perhaps there's some truth to both of your ideas," he said, "but let's order so we won't starve to death before the issue is decided." Old Man Beufort was a Rotarian, a staunch supporter of his local American Legion Post 283, a Kappa and a *cum laude* graduate of Old Miss. Bernard couldn't think of what the poor man had done to deserve Terressa, the fact that there had always been a McCloud on the board of the bank notwithstanding. Fannie stood by the table pad in hand and pencil poised. Bernard liked for her to wait on him because he made passes at her and she turned them down without making too much noise. It had become a game.

"Hello, Lulu," Janice Lorchman said.

"My name's Fannie, mam," the waitress said, smiling good-naturedly.

"Oh yes, Fannie you're my favorite waitress. I'm so glad you're waiting on our party today. I need a drink for Fred. Please bring it quickly or he'll soon start shaking and howling."

"Who's Fred?" Art Reid said.

"It's her alcoholic dog," Terressa explained, pointing to the floor near Janice where a sad-looking poodle lay.

"Isn't he cute," Fannie said. "What's he drink?"

"This time of the day, martinis."

"Of course," Bernard laughed.

"Darling, are you going to order?" Janice asked Terressa.

"Yes. I think I'll have the gumbo. How's your gumbo today, Fannie?"

"Oh, just lovely."

"You shouldn't eat that," Janice said. "There's so much rice in it. It'll make you fat, darling."

"Is the crab or the molded fruit salad the green salad?" Bernard asked.

"We always have one molded salad and one green salad, sir," Fannie said.

"Gracious sakes alive, Bernie," Terressa said, "she has to tell you that every time you come in here."

"I'll take this here trout stuffed with lobster meat," Art Reid said.

While everyone ordered their lunch Janice and Terressa argued over the sorts of small things that become the interest of close friends. "I think I'll have the pistachio ice cream for dessert," Janice said.

"Honey, why don't you have some pecan pie. It's quite Southern. Or haven't you shaken off your Yankee ancestry yet?" Terressa jibed.

The head waiter, Ned, floated over to the table and smiled, showing his upper and lower plates. "Is everything all right?"

"Just fine," Bernard said.

Fannie rushed out of the room to place the order and James stood like a sentinel at the door.

"What were you saying, Janice?" Bernard asked. "Something about man's nature?"

"Oh, yes," Janice said. "The question was whether men are born with inclinations to murder and steal or whether they attain such drives through . . ."

"Not drives, darling," Teressa said. "They should be called dynamics if you believe in that sort of thing . . ."

"Perhaps man is born with certain propensities and attains others," Bernard said.

"They say God gave man two arms and two legs and Socrates to make him rational," Al Mizel said.

"What's that got to do with it?" Janice asked.

"Here, here," Sam Nicholson said. "I believe I know of a case of two brothers right here in this town that will throw some light on this discussion." While he spoke Janice furiously flipped through a book she'd taken from her pocketbook. "Many years ago one of my field workers had a son who developed a genius for hunting, caring for dogs and horses and making things grow. She also had another son whose weakly disposition fit him only for some lowly task such as serving tables or wiping shoes.

"I took it upon myself to encourage the hunter and gave the mother land and money so that her son would train at one of our fine colored agricultural schools and became a prosperous farmer. Well, the ungrateful mother took the money I gave her and the income from the land and put the weakling through high school and then through a Northern college. Now the weakling son's a prosperous and pompous Negro leader in town and I understand the other son just got out of jail."

"Wonderful story," Teressa said.

"It doesn't prove a thing," Janice said.

"It does prove that no matter what a person's natural ability is, his environment affects him greatly," Sam Nicholson concluded.

"Who are you talkin' about?" Al Mizel asked.

"Here, it says right here in this book on the ruling class by Gaetano Mosca that, ' . . . if a certain number of stags are shut up in a park they will inevitably divide into two herds which will always be in conflict with each other. An instinct of very much the same sort seems to make its influence felt among men . . . ,' " Janice said.

"You see," Terressa said, "if man has no basic nature but is conditioned, then the masses of people, right here in this town let's say, can be conditioned to do good. For example we could train them to stop all of the nasty, brutal race-baiting and hating . . ."

"Hell, it'd never work," Art Reid said. "Blacks and whites just weren't made to mix."

After dinner the men went upstairs to the card room, one of the few places in the world they all felt safe to talk truths.

"Ain't no ladies around is there?" Art Reid said before breaking out a new deck of cards and dealing. Bernard, Al and old Sam looked around the room. No one but the bartender and a couple of Negro waitresses were present.

"Who the hell was the nigger you was talkin' about downstairs?" Art Reid asked Sam Nicholson.

"Jacob Blue and his brother Nat who's called Puddin'."

"Whoooeee," they shouted and guffawed.

"How's the election goin'?" Art Reid asked, throwing the question out for general discussion at the card table.

"Doin' a lot o' politickin'," Bernard said. "Floating about a hundred thousand dollars around the state myself."

"Is that right?" Reid said. "You know I didn't come down here just for the insurance commissioners' meeting. Why'd you call me ta come down here from Jackson?"

"You'll see soon enough," Bernard said.

As a child Bernard had heard Art Reid and his paw sit around during hunting season and tell stories of Indians and speak of the slave trade with Africa. He'd been excited as no school book had ever excited him about the living history Art and his paw had talked. You could see in Art's brown neck and red face that he was no idle townsman, and in his keen blue eyes sunken deep in his face there was humor, although Bernard had seen those same eyes looking just as sharp while Art had beat a man to death. That you could never read those eyes was part of the man's attraction. Art was a man of action and you could always count on him to get done what had to be done. He was one of the few whites who'd kill another white as fast as he'd kill a coon and that was no joke.

As Pops, the bartender, served the table a round of mixed drinks, he asked, "How's the election look?"

"Fair," Bernard said.

"What the word on that nigger doctor that's runnin'?"

"Don't know," Bernard said. He was disgusted for he was sure that if white trash like Pops thought Jacob might win, they'd be beating it to his door to ask favors.

"Don't seem right to me," Pops said. "Seems like he ain't got no cause to get so uppity just 'cause he got a little education. Just think o' the disgrace o' us bein' represented in the Congress of these here New Nited States by a black man."

"Lee would turn over in his grave," Bernard said dryly.

"Lee, hell," Pops said. "Even Lincoln didn't want to see no days like this." The table of men laughed. The smell of the den filled Bernard's nostrils. It was one of the best smells he knew; a mixture of liquor, aged wood, pipes and cigars and a damp unnameable cool smell. A rebel whoop came from the lips of a gang of men coming in the door. It felt good to be among the men, slapping them on the back, punching and kidding with them—talking about manly things over drinks and cards.

19

Southern Justice

BERNARD ROSE LATE SATURDAY, taking his time in the shower cleansing the stale perspiration from his body and standing in the steaming stream of the shower trying to drive the last traces of alcohol from his system. Wrapped in a bathrobe Bernard sat on the edge of his bed drawing a cigarette's warm corrosive intoxicating smoke into his mouth-throat-lungs-stomach. Reading the morning paper he realized that the declining price of cotton meant it would be best to sell it at parity to the federal government so that if the cotton market went up the government would sell his cotton and give him the profit. He'd have to check with his agents about foreign markets.

Bernard picked up the phone and dialed the Sheriff's office. "How's things going?"

"Nothin' much. Just a little nigger trouble over in Newtown."

"What happened?"

"Some fella got his throat cut in Fats's Pool Hall."

"Ain't Fats one o' Jacob's men?"

"Yeah."

"This may be a break for us."

"Ya know Fats is a big numbers banker. A lot o' cash goes through his hands."

"Listen. Me and a couple o' friends o' mine will be down there shortly."

Hanging up on the Sheriff, Bernard called the Southern Arms Hotel and spoke to Art. "Yeah, get Al out of bed. I'll be right down to pick you up."

Within half an hour Bernard, Al and Art pulled up behind a couple of Sheriff's cars in Newtown. A large crowd of Negroes gathered on either side of Pearl Street.

"All right, get them all over on the other side of the street," Bernard demanded.

Deputy Hurst and a couple of others began pushing people across the street. Inside Bernard found Fats, a big fellow in work pants and shirt and a filthy homunculus standing near a body that had long been drained of life. Tate was on the phone at the bar. He put the phone down as Bernard approached and nodded.

"Who killed him?" Bernard asked.

"I did, suh," the worker said with a trembling voice.

"D'ja call the undertaker?"

"Yes sir," Fats said.

"Who do you work for, boy?" Bernard asked the worker.

"Mister Tolston," the worker said.

"Boy, don't you know you ought to be in the field?"

"Yas suh."

"Now get out a' heah. We'll take care o' this," Bernard said. The gigantic fellow ran out of the pool hall and disappeared into the crowd on the other side of the street.

"Don't think we don't know about this place," Bernard told Fats. Bernard took his horse pistol out and snapped out the chamber to examine the bullets. Fats started sweating. Closing the chamber Bernard placed the pistol against Fats's head. "You're a bad nigger, ain't ya?"

"No suh," he said.

"Don't lie ta me."

"No suh."

Bernard pushed Fats toward the Sheriff who came down on the man's skull with a club. Fats screamed and ran from the pool hall, knocking Deputy Hurst out of the way as he burst through the front door.

Bernard ran to the front door and shot at Fats as he ran toward the crowd across the street. Women were screaming. Someone threw a brick across the street and it smashed through the pool hall window. Art Reid and Al Mizel suddenly appeared in the middle of the street armed with shotguns blasting away at the crowd.

"A hundred dollars for each one of that fat bastard's teeth," Bernard called above the noise of the street.

Several of the fleeing bystanders, hearing the roar of the gunshots, fell on the street and curled up with their hands over their heads. Art and Al leveled their weapons at the huddled forms and blasted them.

20

Responsible Leadership

BERNARD WAS SEATED at his desk in the warehouse stroking a
cut he'd received when the brick came through the pool hall window when he saw Frailty through the warehouse window. The
Negro hesitated in front of the building and then seemed to
force himself to enter despite his trepidation. Frailty the Republican nigger who swung with any white who'd pay the bill.

Frailty tiptoed across the rug behind Bernard's secretary, who
announced him in a soft voice barely louder than the air-
conditioner and the piped music.

The secretary, who looked like a cut-out from a high fashion magazine, stood by the door with note pad and pencil poised to write. "You may leave, Miss Burbank," Bernard said. Her seeming faithfulness bordered on possessiveness, Bernard thought. He'd have to do something about that problem one day.

"Frailty," he said. "Do sit down."

Frailty shifted his briefcase to his left hand and obediently sat down.

"Did ya take care o' that dead fellow over at Fats's pool hall?" Bernard asked.

"Yes, sir. Another Saturday killing. Every Saturday there's shooting and killing. You'd think those people would learn. I picked up that body out in the street too . . . "

"Oh you did?"

"I don't know why my people don't respect law and order."

"Did you get the papers signed?" Bernard asked.

While Frailty flustered answering and pulled piles of papers from his briefcase, Bernard rose and paced the floor.

"Here's a bank book noting the ten thousand dollar deposit we made to cover that check we wrote you and . . . "

"What check?"

"Why the check for the money you said you needed to give to them fellows in Washington. You said a Washington official would allow our development company to purchase government surplus equipment at cut-rate prices if he was . . . er . . . buttered up a little, so to speak."

"I don't know what you're talking about."

"I got the papers right here signed by everyone who wants to participate. They all contributed money towards . . . "

"Towards what?" Bernard laughed. "I don't know what you're talking about. If you're going to rant and rave you can leave." This new breed of black money-grabbers was curious to Bernard. Without the least background or breeding they expected to buy their way into the most exclusive circles.

"But, Mr. Nicholson, suh," Frailty said. "We have the check. It's proof . . . "

"You probably made the check out to cash," Bernard said. "If there were such a check, anyone could cash it. Besides it's got to go through my bank."

"But sir, you must realize how much this means to our people . . . " Frailty was sweating. The cringing man looked just like Fats did a few hours before with a gun up against his head. There was but one thing Bernard wanted of Frailty at that moment, he wanted the man to tell him of Jacob. What would the bastard try next. The way things stood the Independents had a good chance of winning.

"You think your people will vote for the Democratic Party?"

"Yes, sir, our people are loyal Party people."

"Don't lie, now."

"The development company . . . " Frailty said.

"Now don't worry. If your papers are in order, we'll set it up . . . "

"The ten thousand . . . "

"I tell you I don't . . . " The telephone interrupted Bernard. His secretary answered it in the other room and called him on the intercom.

"It's Judge Clayton," the girl said.

Bernard picked up on the phone.

"How could you?" the Judge said. "Laura's ruined. Have you no respect left for yourself or others?"

"I don't know what to say. I should have called you and told you instead of letting you find out on your own. But there are some things you don't know."

"I've tried so hard to see that Laura was brought up to be a proper Southern lady just like her mother would have wanted."

Bernard looked across his desk into Frailty's eyes; they were eyes that seemed to see nothing and look nowhere. "There's someone here in the office with me now," Bernard said. "But I'll be over to talk to you about this."

"I certainly hope our good name and reputation can be salvaged," Clayton said with a very tired voice. "Also, I've been meaning to talk with you about all this political foolishness goin' on in town but haven't had a chance. I hear there's a riot going on downtown."

"Don't worry," Bernard said. "The Sheriff's handling it."

"I hear some of the Klan's coming into town," the Judge said.

The fact that he'd mention this on the phone meant he disapproved. Bernard wondered what he knew. "Nothin' to that rumor."

"Listen," the Judge said. "The best thing you could do right now would be to go on TV with a Negro leader like Jacob and call for law and order."

Bernard laughed. The idea was so funny he couldn't stop laughing. The Judge was shouting and cursing something on the phone and Frailty was stiffening with fright in his seat in the office. "Goodbye, Judge Clayton," he said and hung up the phone. Bernard leaned back in his chair and reflected for a moment on Clayton's idea. If he, a Whiteman supporter, went on TV with Jacob Blue calling for law and order, the liberals, Justice Department and radicals among the niggers would be completely disarmed. The street fighting would scare a lot of Negroes away from the polls and bring whites in droves. They'd even come from other districts to vote on Monday. They'd have to have a list of dead voters at every poll. His going on TV would cause Negroes brave enough to go to the polls to vote a moderate ticket. And Whiteman, the Democrat, was certainly the moderate compared to Blackstone, the Republican.

"What would you think about a white community leader and a Negro community leader goin' on TV and callin' for law and order?" Bernard asked Frailty.

"I think it would be the responsible thing to do." Frailty clasped and unclasped his sweating hands. "I'd better leave." "I've got another appointment." Frailty rose and let himself out as Bernard began to write up some notes on a desk memo pad.

Suddenly a whistle blew. "That's it," Bernard shouted alone in his office. He ran to the window. On a hill across the river burned a gigantic cross of the Soldiers of the White Christ.

"Mrs. Beufort's on the phone," the receptionist told Bernard.

"Hello, Terressa," Bernard said.

"Bernard. I was just having cocktails with Elizabeth Fletcher and we were talking about flower arrangements and when to use live flowers and when plastic imitations are appropriate and I don't remember why but we started talking about the violence going on and then we heard on the radio or did we hear on the radio about the riot downtown and then started talking about the violence. I do hope the Sheriff keeps the violence down . . . It upsets me so to read the papers these days . . . why Elizabeth was just saying . . . "

Bernard let her talk for a while and then told her, "If the day ever comes that we allow violence to become controlled by the rabble in the streets you can forget about continuing the type of life you live, dear. And it seems that the stupid clods we have entrusted with the means of violence, like our sheriffs, don't know how to use it. Luckily there are some of us who have kept alert waiting for the moment when we would be needed and who are prepared to deal with any sort of violence and to deal out any sort of violence."

"Well, if that's the way you feel, darling," she said feebly.

"I just thought we should be honest."

"Of course, Bernie. Can we expect to see you at the club this evening?"

"I don't know right now. I hope to dine there. Good-bye, Terressa."

The next call was from General Hal Bleumont, promising the official or unofficial support of the state guard if needed. Bernard suggested that he call Mayor Higgins and Senator Whiteman and tell them. He spoke to Anastas Zakis and Ephram Lorchman and found them both terribly concerned that nothing would happen to drive business from their downtown stores or injure their property. They complained that the suburban shopping centers were already taking too much business from them.

2 1

Jacob's Interest in the Matter

RIDING IN THE LIMOUSINE from the airport Jacob heard rumors about some shooting in Newtown. If that particular Saturday night was going to be like other Saturday nights he would be busy and might have to cancel his speaking engagement at New Bethel. The New Orleans meeting on the correction of nutritional deficiencies among the poor had been enlightening; especially so was the speech of a Puerto Rican doctor about her experience in Ghana. She had told the group about what it meant to Ghanaians for the government to put freezers in the fishing boats and to send fish, for the first time, in truck loads up to the mountain villages of the country. As the nutritional level of the villagers rose, so did their mental activity increase in direct proportion. An Indian doctor had talked about the use of the soy bean as a meat and milk supplement and Jacob had talked about the welfare person's diet.

Walking home from the downtown Biltmore where the limousine deposited him Jacob found his usual solitude, enabling him to think about things other than his immediate work.

Shivering with the evening wind at his back he walked downhill past the cotton exchange where cotton prices were marked up on blackboards in white chalk. The faces of the whites in the street seemed to be especially hard that Saturday afternoon. Atop a rise of land Jacob looked behind him and saw the green scummy water of the canal beside the river and the unwinding brown water of the river. His soul was like the river, magnificent from a distance, but upon close examination condums were revealed floating just below the surface and dead babies bobbed along the swift bottom current. Perhaps the directions humans took were no more or less moral than that of the ever-changing river. The land that was once adventurous and romantically beautiful was now broken and fully corrupted like the fat castrated cat that he shared his house with. As first dark approached, the brush beside the road began to breed strange sounds as though the snakes moving through the grass and ants eating at dead trees could be heard.

Appearing without warning was what Jacob at first took to be an apparition, but then he recognized as the wild form of Old Man Gittens. His arms were full of link sausages and pork chops.

"They done gone crazy in town," Gittens said. "Shootin' niggers down in the streets. Stores wide open. Better get yours while the gettin's good . . . " Gittens disappeared into an alleyway and for the first time Jacob noticed a dull yellow glow rising up from the town.

Jacob stopped the first Negro he saw driving a car and directed him to drive him to his home. By the time he reached his house there was a rhythm of gunfire sounding in the town; the shotguns boomed, boomed, boomed, the single shot rifles went bap, bap, bap. The automatic rifles were going bapbapbap-bapbap and there were occasional sounds of explosions, baaarooommmmmmmr

In his clinic, as he feared, Jacob found people bleeding from shotgun wounds in the back and many people suffering from strange wounds whose source was immediately undeterminable.

"My God," Jacob said, seeing the room of frightened injured. "What have we done to deserve this," he whispered to himself. All his life he'd been punished for a crime of an unknown nature. Was it some particular crime against God or fate that had caused his ancestors to be sold into slavery? Was this suffering because of man's original sin? Or was it because he was black?

Luckily Jacob had prepared for trouble on the weekend and had abundant supplies. Before he started he directed Nurse Waters to bare everyone's wounds and to clean them out. Jacob picked up the phone and dialed the Wilsons and asked them to run next door for Jesse.

"Yeah," Jesse said. "I guess you know about what's happening."

"Yes, my office is full of people. Please send some fellows over here who can shoot."

"We will if we can. There's a tank in front of our house in the street right now. We'll do what we can."

"And see if you can direct injured people over here. And get community people to bring bedding, soup and coffee. By the way, I don't think I can make the meeting at New Bethel."

"You must," Jesse said. "We've got to get people organized or we're all lost."

"But I have a commitment right here."

"Damn it, man, this is war, not a school debate."

"You think I don't know. You should see this office."

Jacob hung up and began to operate, digging out shotgun pellets and sewing up gashes and torn skin. Where people had been shot at close range there were nasty burns around the gunshot wounds. Soon people began to come into the office blinded and burnt by tear gas. Its foul smell rose from their clothes causing everyone to cough and their eyes to water.

"Well, Jacob," Jacob heard Bernard tell him on the phone. He hadn't wanted to speak to Bernard but Leah had answered the phone and insisted. "Don't ya think it's about time we put a stop to all this needless destruction and bloodshed?"

"I have nothing to do with it," Jacob said.

"You have everything to do with it," Bernard said nastily. "You have a choice. You can go on TV with Sheriff Tate and Frailty and call for law and order or in thirty minutes you'll be dead or in jail or on the run with the National Guard, the FBI and everyone else looking for you. Within a week we'll have posters for your arrest in every post office in the country."

"I'll let you know," Jacob said.

"You'll let me know right now. I've got a spot on Channel sixteen at eight. You be down at the station."

As Jacob attempted to patch up the torn bodies he was interrupted by Frailty who urged him to be careful and by Strop who insisted that he call the rioters and looters off, as though he were directing the whole thing.

Jacob didn't know exactly when he decided to go down to the station. Perhaps it was during the newscast he'd listened to with the patients.

"This is Wonderful WZNY news. The latest report from Matchez is that the fighting between supporters of the radical Congressional contender Jacob Blue and the police, which started when Negroes fired upon police on Pearl Street, . . . "

"It's a lie. It's . . . " the patients had shouted and booed, but Jacob understood that it made no difference that it was a lie. The whites controlled the instruments of truth-making; the radios and TVs. They controlled the telephones, telegraphs, roads and guns and he knew no way of dealing with that. Jacob laughed to himself as he thought that the meeting at the TV station might be a trick. Perhaps they waited on the road to the station to kill him.

Jacob was still undecided when Schneider came to see him. Nurse Waters told Jacob she'd showed him into the study. Jacob found him there leafing through a magazine.

"Mr. Schneider," Jacob said. "I didn't expect to see you until Monday."

"All the most interesting events will happen before Monday, the way things are going."

"I have nothing to say. You're welcome to stay around and observe," Jacob said. "I'm very busy."

"But not too busy for a TV show?"

Jacob was suddenly frightened by Schneider's sure air. The fellow was a stranger to the town—he'd moved there to teach only a year before—but he spoke as arrogantly as though he were a member of an old aristocratic family. What was the TV show to him?

"To be brief, Jacob. I have information . . . the Justice Department. Their interest is, of course, first of all law and order. But as you might know, they are also concerned about the Dixiecrats straying away from the national democrats. I have been informed by reliable sources that it would be good if you appeared on TV with Sheriff Tate for reasons you can guess."

"I have no interest in your games," Jacob said. "There are seriously injured people here who need attention."

"The point is, Jacob," Schneider said, "you can't afford not to take one hour to appear on that TV show. Otherwise I can't guarantee that your life won't be in danger . . . "

"And if I agree?" Jacob said, infuriated by the blackmail.

"Then you can rest assured that FBI agents, who have infiltrated every political group in this state, will look out for your interests."

Jacob thanked Schneider for his observations and showed him out. As he said goodbye Schneider reminded Jacob, "See you Monday. I am, after all, truly interested in writing a story about your campaign for a national publication.

22

The Blood Ran Deep

As NIGHT THRUST toward Matchez, an undulating whistle sounded over in Louisiana of the kind that might call a spectral army to rise. On the eastern edge of Newtown where cluttered back yards opened to expanses of cotton was a clump of trees. Among these trees was New Bethel Church. Night, running from the East, was met at the edge of town by the gothic New Bethel Church with its spires at once ghoulish and phallic thrusting from the rotting ground to the sky with astonished slit-eyes in the belfry.

Jesse entered New Bethel Church's vestibule and passed Van

Cliffords and Ray Stokes who were talking to several other men dressed in soft clothes barely warp and woof, whose hard hands hung at their sides listening. Van had hung his vest over the head of a clay model of one of the saints. Ray Stokes casually flicked a cigarette into a collection plate.

In the tense meeting room the air was hung with smoke. Below the ceiling, through the smoke, giant wooden beams forming a cross could be discerned. It was commonly known that the beams came from a wrecked river craft. Tacked up over the picture of a Christ was a banner reading "Freedom Now." Flowering from the altar were sprays of microphones. A hastily tacked up spotlight illuminated the stage, washing it in a holy, white light.

Bocat stood atop an aisle talking to J. V. "What happened to Fats?" Bocat asked.

"Well, it was like this," J. V. lied. "Poor Fats went up to a white man, wiggled his thing and the white man shot it off. NBSZ News showed it laying there in the street." They both broke up laughing and holding their sides. When they calmed down, J. V. said, "I'll tell you what we should do. We'll take the president of this country and the president of Russia and put them in an arena to fight. Since they want to fight so bad, let them tear each other's asses up. I'm tired of those mothers sitting in soft chairs and telling thousands of people to go get shot to hell. They throw away lives like you throw away scrap paper so let them get the hell in an arena and kill each other."

The room, choked full of folk from Newtown, Paces Ferry, Blandtown and some from as far away as Griffith, filled with smoke and nervous people taut as piano wire with the knowledge that the town was burning.

Two large Sisters—Mrs. Ella, who worked on the Nicholson's and Vivian, Fats's girl—dressed in white with white gloves, took their places by the doors. Jesse noticed that some families, like the Moores, sat with the women on one side and the men on the other, but most people didn't honor that tradition.

Reverend Grace climbed to the smoky podium and raised his hands. The crowd grew quiet. Grace sat down. Ray Stokes started the cry, "Freedom Now."

The crowd took up the cry, "Freedom Now."

"What do you want?" Brad Wilson chanted like at a football game.

"FREEDOM," hundreds said.

"What do you want?" Dorothy Moore screamed.

"FREEDOM," a chorus of strong voices shouted.

"FREEDOM NOW, FREEDOM NOW, FREEDOM NOW . . . " The church rocked—as it did every Sunday—with holy believers.

Jesse walked into the vestibule and put a quarter in the big, red coke machine beside the saint. The liquid cooled his mouth. The power of the crowd was frightening to Jesse until he realized that this power—whatever power existed, because a couple hundred folk in a small Mississippi town had one mind and one heart—was his power, and he thrilled with that knowledge. Jesse ran back into the meeting shouting, "FREEDOM NOW, FREEDOM NOW, FREEDOM NOW . . . "

All the substantial folk of the area were present—the bootleggers, pullman porters, waiters and waitresses, root women, jackleg preachers . . . Jesse saw Widow Sanders, in the white suit she wore to church every Wednesday and Sunday to shout about sin and salvation, jump up feeling mighty holy and shout, "FREEDOM NOW." And Tina, Dorothy, Puddin' and Bocat were shouting and happy. Their happiness penetrated Jesse and filled him with gladness. Everyone was clapping and it sounded like marching troops and like the roof would tumble down. The pews shook with the clapping, stomping and shouting. The floor shook, the walls shook and the plaster saint in the vestibule, his head covered with Van Clifford's vest, shook. Grace, Fats, and other leaders of the Blue-for-Congress Committee were seated next to the pulpit.

Grace climbed to the podium again and stiffly raised his arms.

After the singing died and the shuffle of people sitting down had stopped, Grace said, standing like a stone figure before the enraptured crowd, "Let us pray." He lowered his bald head and spoke to his protruding stomach. "OHHEAVENLYFATHER-PLEASEBLESSTHESE GOOD PEOPLE, AIDTHEMIN-THEGOODWORKSTHATTHEYAREATTEMPTING. AA-AMEEEEEEEENNNN." He hummed the last word. "Dr. Blue and the other good citizens of Newtown have asked me to put my church at the disposal of you good folk tonight." An unreverent cheer went up, frightening Grace. Wiping the seriousness from his face, Grace suddenly came to life and said, "I have good news for you chillun today."

"Yes sir. Good news," the people shouted back.

"I say good news. Freedom is a'coming. And those lost souls that afflict this town will be soothed."

"Amen."

"The children have wandered in the wilderness too long. I'm speaking to you today because the whole land is troubled." Grace's voice rose to dramatic proportions. "We are walking in the valley. We are DEEP in the shadow of death." He almost whispered "shadow." Jesse found the speech amusing because Grace had opposed the organization in its early stages but as it became powerful and he found it could provide an audience for him, he was all for it.

"Amen . . . Yessir . . . tell it."

Softly he said, "Death clouds the sky from my eye. Death's dark shadows strike the land from my eyesight. Death is on every hand. To the North. To the South. It comes from strangers and friends. It comes from those bearing gifts.

"Today I want to warn you children. Beware of those who come to you as friends but are your enemy. False friends will lead you to the fires of an earthly hell. They want to see your bodies writhe in the fires of racial hate and have the tongues of intolerance lap up your body. Those devils would feed the fires. But they are merciful, you say. I am here to tell you that the mercy of the devil is cruel. Who will comfort you in the valley of the shadow of death? The harbingers of violence? The enemies of the South? No! Rely upon those of us who know you and have lived with you and loved you. I tell you this not out of hate for the devil but out of love for our beautiful community . . . "

The audience murmured. Widow Sanders asked Tina Moore, "What's he talking about?"

" . . . then shall goodness and mercy follow you all the days of your lives. I say we must put our trust in the government and we must appeal to the conscience of the land for help."

"The government put us in this trick," Curtingham Korney shouted.

"The conscience of the good people never stopped a lynching," Van Cliffords shouted.

Grace leaned from the pulpit and whispered to the deacons nearby and spoke to Reverend Broom from Mt. Zion. Then he announced, "Jacob Blue has been delayed. Until he's able to get here—I believed he's attending to those wounded in the shooting downtown—we'll hear from Jesse Haines, a fellow we've all gotten to know real well during the past months."

Jesse jerked himself up from his seat and moved to stand erect in the spotlight, passing Grace who was on his way down to his seat. Jesse set his jaw and stuffed his hands down in the pockets of his wrinkled denim suit.

Cameras rolled. Jesse saw the placid faces of Kuetner, Lowman and the other newsmen in the front row. Church fans in black hands anxiously whirred. "As you know," Jesse said, "newsmen and town officials have said we're responsible for the rioting now going on in the town. Well, we're not going to talk about the responsibility, that's obvious, just ask Fats here who they tried to shoot down outside his own establishment like a dog, or talk to some of the people who were shot in the back running from the police. It was the police who rioted, not us."

Jesse frowned and said, "We've been buked and scorned too long."

The congregation before him shouted with violent love, "Yes, Yessir, . . . too long . . . Jesus. Tell it."

"We're going to talk about getting ourselves right. You know the story of Jesus?" he asked with a staccato rhythm above all the shouting. The woofing voices died.

"Once on the Sabbath Jesus plucked ears of corn to eat. But the Pharissee said that it was unlawful to pick corn on Sunday."

"Watch it. Preach." The people, sweating shoulder to shoulder in familiar seats, moved as one body. A movement in one part of the congregation worked its way like ripples on a pond to all other parts. Invisible bonds pulled people together and toward the stage. Faces strained with smiles. The white faces in the church, like drops of white paint in black, were now lost from Jesse's sight.

"Jesus ate on Sunday."

"Yes he did," Fanny shouted.

"Jesus healed the sick on the Sabbath although it was not legal."

"Tell it," the people chanted.

"What we want is freedom," Jesse said, uncloaking the essence of his speech from religious wrappings. "We must have it today. If it's illegal for us to have it today—we're gonna have it anyway. That's what Jesus would do."

The men laughed deeply and the women covered their mouths lady-like and snickered. Tina's pudgy body rolled and trembled with laughter and her head bobbed up and down in agreement. "Make it plain, Jesse."

Jesse anxiously sought the eyes of his audience for approval. He waited for a stream of murmuring conversation to run down to a whisper. "Now I'm going to tell you something you can't read in history books. Something police spies and good white folks in the audience don't know." The crowd was in a good mood. A baby cried out and Jesse wondered if Rachel were in the church with Dan. "The first man to fall in the American revolution was a black man—Crispus Attucks," he said. "Why should the black man have given his blood in the American revolution when America meant slavery? Slavery was written into the Constitution. Did you know that the Constitution of the United States says we're three-fifths of a man?" Jesse paused to flourish his handkerchief and mop his brow.

"Foreign wars among Europeans made it possible for Haitians to revolt. Wouldn't this have been an excellent time for Black Americans to strike? To tear down all those gods placed over us to rule us? Denmark Vessey tried it in South Carolina but his remarkable plot was betrayed, it wasn't coordinated with plots throughout the land." Jesse walked to the side of the podium and stood on a narrow ledge of a step, balancing himself with one had slightly touching the lectern. "Instead the black man was taught to love, to be meek, to be pure in heart, to be persecuted, to be dead and the lost of the earth." A roar swept through the church like the sound of falling water. Lowman, the racist, turned with fright to Kuetner, the liberal, who sat listening without emotion, and said, "That's treason!" And Kuetner said, "You found what you came for then."

Jesse pointed to the statue of the bleeding thin man crucified on the cross on the wall. "What's that man done for you? Has that graven image put food on your table? Given you seeds to sow? Harvested your crops?"

Squawking and fretting like fighting cocks, Grace and his deacons furtively whispered and furiously looked to Jesse. Grace climbed to the podium and mumbled a plea into Jesse's ear. A current of murmurs swirled and eddied through the congregation.

"I will not be allowed to continue speaking in this house of God," Jesse announced with all the hurt dignity he could muster. "Anyone who wants to hear the rest of my talk please step outside. Come out from under this cross," he beckoned, pointing to the smoky rafters. J. V.—rifle in hand—ran to

Jesse's side and proudly walked with him from the church. The crowd was silent and then they slowly took careful steps out of the church and into the yard. In the Mississippi night they could see the Sheriff and his men parked down at the entrance to the churchyard.

"You must leave," Grace said. "You can't meet here." The crowd booed, hissed and shouted him down. Frailty came up the road and whispered in Grace's ear. They both walked back down the road to the Sheriff.

"They didn't say a word about the evictions," Puddin' said. He went through the crowd, gathering his family to leave. Fats saw him and asked, "Please let me ride out o' here in your car. I'll hide on the floor. If they catch me here, it's all over."

Puddin' screwed his face up like he was eating something bitter and left the crowd with Fats. Jesse watched Puddin' drive down the road, stop for a moment and talk to the Sheriff and then head for Newtown.

When the churchyard was filled with people who trespassed upon old graves, and the new mounds of earth—the same dirt the people worked in the fields and that sifted through their shacks—became vantage points for the viewers, Jesse began. "That Son of God hanging on that cross in that church," he shouted, "has given you nothing. He's promised you everything, just as the schools and welfare people have promised you everything." Charging Jesse, a reporter poked a portable tape-recorder mike at him. "If we're going to be free, we must do it ourselves. Isn't that right?" No one answered. "I know what this means. Don't you think I know what this means. This is serious business, this business of freedom. Follow me and I promise you nothing but struggle and hate and death, a significant death. You're going to die of consumption and anemia and lynching anyway. I know what forces my speech will set in motion. But we'll not be the losers. This land that torments us will be the loser."

"FREEDOM, FREEDOM, FREEDOM," the cry arose.

"Eeeeiii . . . "

"The dogs . . . "

"Cops . . . "

People screamed. The police turned spotlights on the disintegrating crowd. Walking silhouetted in the light Jesse could see men handling the dogs. Fannie Randolph ran past, her wig at a forty-five-degree angle. The dogs leaped forward, free of their leashes. A gun barked. Bang. Bam. Bam. The dogs fell. It was J. V., picking them off with his rifle. Jesse, his back wet with perspiration and his skin alert and tingling with danger, started moving toward the church. Tiny explosions popped around Jesse and the smothering fumes of tear gas spead toward his face. Jesse yelled, "Put handkerchiefs to your faces."

"There's that nigger," someone shouted. A light flashed and Jesse jumped back around the side of the church. A blast from a shotgun swished past like the wings of a giant bird.

Jesse pulled out his .38 and fired at the spotlight. It went out with a crash. Someone near it screamed in pain. Jesse ran through the graveyard, jumped a stone fence and headed through the woods. Briars tore at his clothes and skin. He seemed to pass miles of roads and fields. Whenever he neared a farmhouse dogs would bark and sometimes a light would be turned on. He sensed that he was near the river as he ran through a junkyard full of stacks of the skeletons of cars. Running through a damp field with cat-o-nine-tails brushing against him, he had the hallucination that those dried hulks were the souls of all the dead Indians and Negroes whose blood ran deep in the ground fertilizing it. He throught he could hear the rushes and broomstraw in the field calling his name. Nearing the town he cut through a lane. Mrs. Gunther was throwing slops into her back yard. As Jesse jumped her fence he felt absurd and said, "How do." The old lady waved good-naturedly, hunched up her shoulders and went back to her house. After stumbling, groping and floundering along the road and in the fields Jesse saw a bunch of lights that he reasoned had to be Camp Grove Lane. Everything he'd known in his life was unimportant to him at that moment compared to his own black life. Just like in the city jail, he discovered once more that he was black and small and nobody cared. Neither laws nor religion nor morals could help in the end when the matter was his own black life.

"Halt," someone commanded.

Jesse dashed forward. He was so close. A shot thundered. The light of the rifle revealed a black face.

"That's a warning."

Why shouldn't the hand to take his life be black, Jesse thought. The whites had hired a black to do the job.

"Jesse?" a husky voice asked.

May the devil take his soul. "Yes."

"Good to see you. Almost shot you."

Jesse recognized Bocat. "Where's your paw?"

"Over at Mrs. Gittens' place. When you see them tell 'em it was me what was shootin'."

Jesse knocked at the door. The lights went out in the front room. "Who is it?" Widow Sanders said.

"Jesse," he whispered.

The house had the same strange odor about it he'd noticed the night before. The shades, which were kept down during the day to keep the sun from ruining the furniture, were now pulled to hold the light inside. Evidently everyone was in the front room that was full of tall-backed, flower-decorated, stuffed and cushioned Louis XIV chairs, tiffany lamps, tables crowded with porcelain figurines of the Holy Family, plaster dogs and cats and a TV.

He followed her through the hallway full of coon tails, stuffed birds, dried animal skins, pots with incense burning and other paraphernalia to impress her customers, into the front room. There, Tina, Puddin', Fats, Elizabeth and Dot sat about the TV.

"We heard on TV what happened after we left the church," Tina said.

Jesse dropped into a chair.

"You all right, boy?" Widow Sanders asked.

She fetched a bowl, an antiseptic and a towel and started to clean up the scratches on Jesse's face and hands. She put a sheet on the chair so he wouldn't get it dirty. Although he offered to sit on the floor, she insisted that he sit there.

"And now BQW-TV presents a special public service feature. We have a special announcement to be made by Sheriff Tate, John Frailty and Jacob Blue," said a young boyish-looking announcer on the screen.

"That son-o-bitch," Fats said. "What they can't do themselves they can always get a colored man to do . . . "

" . . . I hope the respectable nigra . . . ," Tate was saying.

"He can't even say 'Negro,'" Jesse said.

"Quiet," Dot said.

" . . . will help us drive the rotten elements out of our town who have been sent here to stir up trouble . . . "

"Thank you, Sheriff," the announcer said. "Now for a word from Congressional contender Jacob Blue . . . "

"Friends." Jacob looked tired. "I have lived and worked with you all my life. We all know that things are not as they should be in Matchez. Life for many of our people is just plain rotten. But we must not be driven by our frustration to acts of violence. We must let the Sheriff's office and the Justice Department, if need be, conduct an investigation of events downtown today which led to several Negroes being shot in the back and feet . . . "

"How can the Sheriff investigate when he's the one who did it?" Fats asked.

"Shhhh," Widow Sanders shushed.

" . . . we must work together with the good white citizens of Matchez to . . . "

"The only good one is a dead one," Fats said.

"Turn it off," Jesse said.

"What we goin' ta do now?" Widow Sanders asked. "Our big leader done gone over to the white folks' side?"

"I knows what I'm goin' ta do," Puddin' said. "I'm gettin' out o' this here rat hole fast as that car'll carry us . . . "

"It's a shame, shame, shame, shame, tch, tch . . . mmmmmmmmmmm. It's a shame," Widow Sanders said.

"What's that?" Jesse said.

"Here this boy's Jacob Blue's big brother and he's been kicked out o' his house, been jailed fo' nothin' and Jacob is runnin' around with white folks livin' big."

"I'm what?" Puddin' said.

"You're Jacob's brother. Don't you remember playin' wid him when you was young?"

"Yeah. But I never knew. How come he become a doctor?"

"I don't know. You goin' ta have to ask Anne. You allus thought that I raised ya and your ma was dead, but it ain't so."

"You go tell Jacob his brother is comin' to see him," Puddin' said. "But first I got somethin' ta do. C'mon," he called, and everyone followed him out of the house.

"What ya going to do?" Jesse asked Puddin'.

Puddin' grabbed an axe from the chopping block in the yard and started toward his house. Whunk, whunk, the axe sounded. Puddin' pulled planks from the side of the house. Understanding what he was about, everyone joined Puddin'. Dorothy tore at the joists of the house with a steel bar. Fats ripped into the porch with a club fashioned from a log. Neighbors came from their houses and stood watching for a while and then went back inside to get their own axes. They joined Puddin' tearing at the house.

"If'n they won't let us live in decent houses," Puddin' shouted as he threw a last brick into the darkness of the yard, "then they ain't goin' ta have no houses ta collect rent on." Jesse was wet with perspiration and exhausted.

As Fats, Jesse, Dorothy, Tina and Elizabeth and Puddin' climbed into their car, a police car swerved into the lane, speeding past them.

Its siren blared and died out as it skidded into Puddin's empty yard. Two white men jumped from the car, guns drawn. Jesse could hear them shouting.

"I told you there'd be trouble . . . " one said.

"That's Nicholson," Dot told Jesse.

Jesse recognized the other man; it was Deputy Hurst.

"What's goin' on here," Hurst asked the crowd of neighbors.

"Nothin'," a fellow said.

"Someone's stole my house," Nicholson wailed. "Where's my house?" he shouted, staring at the bare spot where the shack once stood.

"We always told you that house was goin' ta fall down, boss," someone said.

"Search them," Nicholson ranted.

"Now hold on, Bernard . . . "

Puddin' let the car roll down the lane. At the end of Camp Grove Lane, Bocat jumped in the car and they started the engine.

23

Breaking Invisible Barriers

How could such a thing happen? Jacob wondered. Was it possible for a man to grow up and take root right next to another man and not realize he was his brother? At first he didn't believe Widow Sanders. But he was forced to believe it by the memory of the passage in the Bible. He thought the entry "Nat 1925" was about some relative's child—not his brother. And then the fearful thought that, after all, they had been born into a slave state where the families of blacks were no more sacred than that of cattle . . .

"He say he's comin' here," Widow Sanders said.

"Be glad to see him," Jacob said. "Be glad to see him. What do you think's on his mind?"

"Can't tell with Nat."

"Well you run and try and meet him," Jacob said. "And tell him to bring his family here. It'll be safer here than at his place."

Jacob felt that he was, all of a sudden, facing a test of his substance as a man in a trial as demanding as a wrestling match with an angel. While most people remained safely tucked away in one world or another like the designs and figures trapped inside the marbles of children, in his life he'd be forced to break from one crystal-hard world into another and another. He would always work at scratching away the invisible, rock-hard material separating him from Frailty, Grace, Jesse, Strop and Stokes, Curt and the rest. He would continue until he could look at all of them with the honesty that he knew when he looked at a girl lying naked next to him after making love.

Strangely, as though portending some tragic event, people stopped coming into his clinic with torn, burnt and broken bodies. He went back around to all of the patients and checked them over again, ordering Nurse Waters to change the dressing in some cases. Several of the patients were strange people who'd heard about the ruckus and who'd come in from the rurals to see about it. Finally Jacob got around to treating J. V., who said he'd just sprained his ankle and who limped from window to window. But when he went to examine the ankle J. V. drew back.

"What is it?" Jacob asked.

"Nothin'," J. V. said. He opened his big World War II campaign jacket. Hanging from a rope sewn into the jacket was a carbine with a long sixteen-shot clip. "Jesse sent me over. He said you wanted a guard."

Jacob laughed and patted J. V. on the back. "I feel much more at ease. I'd thought Jesse wasn't able to do it."

J.V. closed up his coat and resumed hopping from one end of the house to the other.

When Frailty came into the house, Jacob led him into the study where he plopped down into a soft leather chair.

"What's the problem?" Jacob asked. The glass crystal around Frailty's world seemed hard as ever, but Jacob detected a crack. Perhaps if he shouted Frailty would hear him. "Hell of a mess!"

"I . . . hate . . . them." Frailty said.

Jacob poured him a drink. Frailty's crystal cocoon was crumbling about him. And Jacob felt comfortable with Frailty for the first time. Now he was a man who had weaknesses, who grew tired, disgusted and who perspired, ruining his starched collar and who smelled with the odor that fright stimulates in men.

"What is it?" Jacob asked.

"Bernard stole the ten thousand from me. But it isn't just like that. It's a whole lot of things. Like they want me to ignore the bodies that are coming into the funeral home. Business as usual. And it's that they want me to arrest Negroes. Just Negroes."

Jacob downed a jigger of brandy. Frailty went to the TV and flicked it on. Jacob knew he'd slipped back behind the steel-hard invisible barrier. They watched the news describe the riot in town in between an account of a rape and something about the war. Jacob left Frailty and found Jeanne to instruct her to prepare sandwiches, coffee and any other food she could put quickly together for the guests that were expected.

"EEEEiiii," someone screamed from the front room.

A woman ran into Jacob pointing toward the clinic. Amid the suffering and frightened people Jacob found Strop with his wife in his arms. Jacob took the woman, whose party dress was stained with blood and placed her on a bench. "What happened?" he asked.

With glassy eyes staring straight forward Strop said, "We were coming from dinner at the Biltmore. Waiting for a cab on the street. A jeep drove up and a man shot her. Didn't say a word. Allemena screamed, 'I'm shot,' and the bastard said, 'Well lay down and die, nigger.' Please help her, Jacob."

The woman was obviously dead, but Jacob picked her up and took her into a treatment room and locked the door so no one could see the outrage. He didn't need a bunch of wailing mourners in the house.

Jacob helped his mother into the study where Puddin', Tina, Dorothy, Elizabeth, Bocat, Jesse, Widow Sanders and Fats sat eating sandwiches and coffee. Frailty had pulled himself up close to the TV. As Jacob held his arm about his mother he was afraid. He'd always been afraid of the warm deep-running force that responded electrically to his mother's touch. Jacob felt as nervous as when he was young in the church smelling of flowers where, pounding and jumping on the floor, he stood whole with the eyes of his mother and friends praising his nakedness before the Lord. The warmth of his mother's body next to his was the same warmth he'd felt in church during his youth on that day when the Ghost had taken his body and possessed it and the brown faces of all the men had smiled on him. He thought he'd forgotten those days, but they were coming back to his mind in flashes that were as real as the experience itself had been.

"Have a chicken sandwich," Tina said to Dorothy.

"No thanks, Ma. I done had a couple o' ham sandwiches."

"Won't you have a little more coffee, dear?" Widow Sanders asked Fats.

"It's true," Anne said as a way of introducing the problem they had to grapple with.

There was a moment of silence.

"What can I do?" Jacob asked.

Silence followed silence.

Charging in her typical manner into the room Leah asked, "What's everyone so glum about. We should celebrate something like this. It isn't every day . . ."

"Shut up," Jacob said.

"It's too late," Puddin' said. "Our lives is about done wid. I just wants ta get ta Memphis or maybe Chi' . . ."

"I know some people in Memphis who . . ." Leah blurted.

"Shut up, I said," Jacob yelled. "Do you remember a straw hat with a leather brim we always fought about?" Jacob asked Nat.

"Yeah. Ragged old thing. Weren't worth a fight. But we sure got it on."

"Remember when you come from playing in the fields hungry and sold me this ring for a quarter?" Jacob asked, extending his hand. There, tightly wed to his second finger, was a simple worn metal band.

Anne gave a startled cry. "I wondered how you got to hold of it," she said. "It were you pa's."

"I've got to talk to you alone," Jesse said, grabbing Jacob around the shoulders. They walked into a small anteroom. As they closed the door to the study he heard Anne tell Leah, "Nat were the strongest and bravest, but I always seemed to see something special about Jacob . . ."

"I'm leaving tonight," Jesse said.

Angrily Jacob argued, "How can you do that? How can you come into a town, build up people's hopes, get them involved in deadly things and then leave?"

"The police know me . . . they'll kill me on sight. I'm no more use here. It's up to you and the organization we've set up."

"The police will stop us too." The quiet of the closet-sized room was frightening.

"No, Jacob. After your TV appearance, they think they've got you in their hip pocket. Just remember, Jacob. Don't cut yourself off."

"Off from what?"

"Your roots."

The door opened and Rachel and Curt crowded into the cubicle. Rachel spit at Jacob's feet and stormed out. Rachel was gone. The woman he'd met through Jesse at a bar, the woman who he knew was certain had only been a laugh at something he'd taken seriously, an efficient lover whose hips drew life from him and exploded it from her womb. They had shared a hatred for their enemy, their favorite drinking toast had become, melodramatically, "death to our enemies." He knew then he needed more—he needed Leah who meant appointments kept, the correct papers signed, meeting the right people, doing the smart things.

"She believed in you," Jesse said. "She put you above all other men. That TV show was quite a shock."

"You're all a bunch of irresponsible romantics," Jacob said, intent upon pulling the last layer of deafening, deathening cover from everyone around him.

Curt looked into Jesse's face and they were quiet. Then Jesse said, "I am a poor man. A simple man. A man of the earth. I was born not too far from here and I've traveled the world over. I have returned to the land of my birth to fight for my people. My teeth point out my basic problem," Jesse said. "For the eight years I've been in this struggle, everyday I've awakened to look at my teeth rotting a little more. But I know that I can't take the time or money to get them fixed until I'm able to live as a whole man."

"I know a dentist in New Orleans. I was just speaking to him earlier today. I'll fix you right up."

"Can you fix up everyone in town?"

"But you must be healthy to even conduct a fight. At the meeting this morning on nutrition . . ."

"Where'd you hold the meeting?"

"In New Orleans."

"No, I mean what hotel? I'll tell you. You held it in the Ambassador Hotel that cost your organization of doctors fifty thousand dollars for the entire week. With that type of money you could have started building a hospital. You could have sent a team of doctors . . ."

"You couldn't get those doctors together in any other place," Jacob argued. He was determined to crack the hard shells about Curt and Jesse that made everything they said half-truth or absurdity to him.

Curt handed Jesse a TWA bag from which Jesse pulled coveralls and low-cut boots. As he spoke to Jacob he placed a blue polka-dot handkerchief around his head and pulled the coveralls on. "Puddin' is sittin' out there alive, right?" Jesse asked. "Alemena is in that other room dead, right? Well the reason that raggedy little man in there who you just discovered was your brother is alive is because of his nigritude. You can look for all the principles you want but he's got 'em all—all what's needed. He can scrape and bow or he can fight like hell. That's what you need to survive in America."

"What will happen on Monday?" Jacob asked.

"Win or lose, there'll be little difference. The greatest changes have already been made. We've done what we could here," Curt said.

"I need two things from you. Give me more of these," Jesse said, handing Jacob a bottle. "Or perhaps some dexedrine. They'll keep me awake for three days. You understand."

Jacob found the medicine Jesse wanted and shook hands with him. He didn't want him to leave. "Where are you going?" he asked.

"I hear there's a little work up in Memphis, boss," Jesse laughed.

As they reentered the study, Jacob noticed Jesse had the smile on his face that he so detested among the movement people. They were either fighting mad or cracking idiot smiles and seemed completely to lack a range of normal human moods which included pathos, irony, shock and more.

"God has brought us all together once again," Anne said as Jacob walked through the room.

"The TV just said Laura, Clayton's niece, is going to hand out Thanksgiving turkeys at the Nicholson's place to the poor," Frailty called to Jacob. An announcer on the TV seemed to be discussing how to prevent riots. "The announcer says . . ."

"Isn't that nice of Miss Laura," Leah said.

"No, it isn't nice. They've stole from us for so long they got enough to give away . . ." Dot argued.

Nurse Waters called Jacob.

"Look it Jesse," Elizabeth shouted.

"Hush up, baby," Tina said, looking at the man Elizabeth pointed to.

"You mind if a worker looking for a job travels along with you folk to Memphis?" Jesse asked.

"Lands sakes alive. It be Jesse," Tina said.

Everyone stared.

Nurse Waters called Jacob again and he started toward the clinic thinking of Frailty, a man caught between two worlds or standing between two worlds or perhaps running furiously between two worlds; Jesse, who flip-flopped from one world to another and then fell off a ledge into a third world and fell up; and Puddin' and all the rest of the people who were cast into a frightening chrysalis of silence. Jacob realized at that moment that he'd fought with an angelic power that had marked him forever and that the struggle he'd engaged in had changed him unalterably.

In the clinic someone turned on a portable radio and music bounced from the walls. He laughed, for most doctors he knew played light classics. In his office the patients had tuned a radio one of them sported like a prize from the fair to a rhythm-and-blues station.

J.V. ran into the clinic, the compact, ugly rifle in his hand. "The tank's coming," he whispered to Jacob. They both went to the window and watched the shadows in the street.

"Is it cold out?" Jacob asked.

"Yeah," J.V. said, his eyes searching the street.

They could hear the grinding of a heavy truck motor. Jacob didn't want to die. He looked at the people in the room. Most had extra coats and dresses pulled over them. The new clothes branded them as looters. Because of that, among other things, death was a real possibility.

Jacob had come to that point in life without signposts to guide him. He realized just how precarious the venture called life really is. So many decisions were made before he was born by people he didn't know. So many lives were affected by his. People he'd never know.

He considered whether the men he'd known were good or bad? Was Schneider good or bad? Bernard? Frailty? Jesse? Jacob? Whether you were good or bad during your life is what his mother would tell him counted when the grim reaper faced you. But he didn't really care at that moment. He had had such a simple purpose. And now he might be forced to choose martyrdom. But in the confusion that would follow his death, the confusion of distorted reports in the press, his choice might never be known. Jacob swore that if he lived, he would never be so simple again as to think that he could fight for the form of anything without considering the all-important essence of the thing he wanted. He would never say we must fight for the right to vote or right to blow bubbles or right to anything. For the right to vote and all rights are related to so many other things. He might even live to see his hope realized, but he knew now that he would also see created from his own effort forces and events that he wouldn't recognize or be able to deal with.

When the machine pulled to a stop in front of Jacob's house, he almost cursed out J.V. for calling an armed personnel carrier a tank, but then knew what an absurd position that would put him in. They could both do the same job.

A white man in a green helmet and gas mask over his face poked his head out of a hatchway in the machine. Jacob could see several machine guns pointing at his house from holes in the carrier. The man removed his gas mask and called to another fellow in the carrier who also stuck his head out. The metallic sound of a two-way radio came from the carrier. The two seemed to be laughing and pointing at Jacob's house. They replaced their masks and the tank rolled down the street and out of the neighborhood. It was moving toward Newtown.

Jacob faced the black silence of the street.

"J.V.," Jacob called to the fellow beside him. His fear had caused him to shout.

"Who?"

Was he going mad? "You. Can you get over to Newtown and warn people to stay in their homes?"

"We got a radio car near here. It'd be easier to . . ."

"It's up to you, J.V.," Jacob said.

"My name's not J.V."

"Since when?"

"Since today. You can call me Raz X. I've given up my white name . . ."

As Raz ran out the front door Jacob noticed Grace's presence. The man rested his hand on the shoulder of one of the people from the rurals who'd come into town when news of the riot spread and somehow caught some buckshot. A strange sort of strength flowed from the hand to the face of the patient. When Jacob saw Widow Sanders furiously praying he knew that somehow the word about Mrs. Strop's body in the treatment room had gotten out. Next to her Elizabeth sat swinging her arms and, oblivious to everyone in the room, sang, "Who's goin' down in der grave wid me? Oh Lawd, who's goin' down in da grave wid me? Jesus goin' . . ." And Strop was crying, face in hands.

"Thank God it's quieting down," Jacob whispered to Nurse Waters.

"God, what will they do?" she said.

"Who do?"

"The ones who won't come?"

"I don't have time for riddles," he said, his temper getting short and hot.

"Ain't no reflection on you doctor. But most people what's getting hurt wouldn't dare come here . . ."

"I don't understand. We'll treat the folk."

"But they still won't come," she said.

"Nonsense," Jacob said. How could people fear him? After all he'd done. Everyone knew that he didn't push anyone to pay a bill they couldn't afford.

Epilogue

THE JEW AT THE GROCERY STORE had told Jacob of the strange men asking about him. His fear had caused him to move in an ever-tightening circle closer and closer to home. At some points during the week after the failure of his campaign he'd become too frightened to leave one room and enter another. Finally, the only thing that kept him going was the knowledge that he was preparing for a moment of truth in a time when a lie was an easy thing.

Jacob laughed as the radio broadcast a New York program about the war. In the cold night the reception was good and stations thousands of miles away tuned in clearly. The announcer, who, Jacob was convinced, was speaking directly to him, said, "It is hard to win a war and be humanitarian. In Vietnam we are attempting both and failing to accomplish either. American forces today bulldozed a village of eighteen hundred and moved the unappreciative villagers thirty miles south to a hamlet. The general in charge of the operation said that the unusual humanitarian gesture would lose us fewer friends in the end but that the villagers didn't seem thankful to the good-naturedness of the American forces.

"It was reported that forty Viet Cong were caught trying to flee the village and were killed . . ." The voice faded out. So we were fighting an humanitarian war? Jacob laughed hopelessly to himself. " . . . when the bombs hit it looked just like the Fourth of July . . ." Jacob's body shuddered and he flicked off the radio.

Perhaps he'd lost because they were masters of evil and deviltry. After two days of such thoughts while seated alone in his study seeing no one, Jacob wondered if these thoughts were motivated by the stimulant he was taking to stay awake, by his fear, or if they were based on reality.

It wasn't until the call from Ethel Wisner the night before the election that Jacob had any hint of the divisive forces working against him.

"Jacob," she'd said, long and cool with her sweet round Southern drawl. She uttered one word and he knew who it was. "It's me, Ethel. Ah just wanted ta thank ya fo' what you did ta keep our town safe from anarchy."

"I just did what any sane person and citizen would be expected to do," Jacob said.

Then she had said, "Ah'd lak ya to come ta our class on contemporary world problems and talk about anything ya want ta talk about . . ."

"Well, you know I'm very busy right now but perhaps after the campaign."

"Ya know you've got my vote, Jacob," she'd said, "but I'm

afraid a lot of whites who were goin' to vote for ya are mighty confused. Why Janice Lorchman's maid told my maid that Mrs. Lorchman's spreading the word around the town that your brother is a convict called Nat something or other and that you got a girl down on Water Street. I don't really care but it's such a damned nuisance to have come up during election time. But yes I do care. Now I'm willing to tolerate a lot of things and you know I'm behind you but adultery and bad birth are just a bit too much. Is any of that talk true?"

"I don't know . . ." Jacob had whispered.

"How thoroughly disappointing. I mean how could you not know? I hear Elizabeth Fletcher told Lucy Tilly that she has evidence that you're positively lecherous and that you've got girls all over town. Now you know how much I care about ya Jacob, but . . ."

"Is that all people are saying?"

"Well, ah hear the men in town are awful concerned that you have criminal connections. Somehow they got hold of some of your fingerprints and they're sending them ta Washington ta see if you've got a criminal record. I assume nothin' will come of that. Now what do you say about speaking ta our class?"

"Be glad to speak to your class about my experience with dem-o-cratic pol-i-tics or perhaps the truth about the American heritage or something to that nature as soon as there's time."

When he'd cradled the white telephone in its receiver Jacob was startled by Jeanne's saying, "What's a poll watcher, Mr. Blue?"

He'd assumed that he'd been alone in the study. When he heard Jeanne's voice he immediately went through his actions of the previous moment to decide if she'd seen or heard anything embarrassing or that should be explained. "A poll watcher watches voting polls. Why?" he asked her. No, there was nothing he'd said that needed explaining.

"Well, Mr. Whiteman asked me if'n I'd poll watch fo' him and ah said yes."

"Whiteman spoke to you?"

"No. But Mr. Frailty told me what Mr. Whiteman told him to tell me."

"Listen, honey," Jacob told the girl. "You tell all your friends that've been hired to poll watch to make sure and get their free lunch and pay before the election's over. And about watching. The only thing you have to watch is the clock to make sure Whiteman doesn't cheat you out of your wage."

While watching Jeanne leave the room, rather awkward after their short encounter, Jacob wondered if those who live under an evil system must participate in it fully, or otherwise run the risk of being jealous of those who like Frailty, Bernard or Raz were without reservation committed to evil and successful in their pursuit. Jacob thought of how easy it seemed for the good citizens of the town to take the name of a citizen and attach to it the most succulent evils. So people now thought that he was from a long line of criminals and a danger to the town's women? Why couldn't he be like those powerful men who were evil and at the same time looked upon as good, holy and lawful in the eyes of the townfolk? That was the position to envy, the position of men like the Nicholsons or Claytons.

The night before the election, the radio and TV had intensified their attack. On the "Sunday Evening News"—regarded by Matchez folks as the voice of truth—Jacob heard a reporter say, "The latest development in the hot race in the seventh congressional is that voters are reacting critically to revelations of Jacob Blue's secret private life. Listen to our nine o'clock news for inside information on the scandal that's causing heads to roll in Matchez, Mississippi. Listen for the details of Jacob Blue's most unusual personal life."

Jacob had lost: 21,567 for Whiteman and 20,619 for him. Jesse, Bo, Nat, Tina, Dot and Elizabeth were safe in Memphis. They'd called him upon their arrival Sunday morning. That call had brought down upon him a loneliness so heavy he didn't know how he'd bear up. It reminded him that the political campaign with all its mud-slinging had little meaning when placed beside the fact that he knew Old Man Nicholson had had his paw killed and there was no way that he could punish him. There was no way he could outrage people about that outrage. During the days that followed the election whenever he chanced to doze off white-sheeted killers ran through his mind.

Widow Sanders, true to character, spread truths, half-truths and gossip about Jacob and Nat to whoever would listen. Mrs. Rowe told him that she'd heard from her root woman (none other than Widow Sanders) that Jacob had paid off his brother to leave town after trying to hide him unsuccessfully from the town during the previous twenty or thirty years. Actually the rumor had been inspired by Widow Sander's witnessing Jacob giving Nat a few dollars to help him get on his way to Memphis.

With his business slackening, Jacob finally came to spend most of his time in his study. He looked around the room full of space, with two of its high walls holding large impressive paintings. One was a water color with a lot of toned-down blue and red forming simple lines that suggested a crowd of people who seemed to be hailing a leader. It was an experiment with materials, lines and colors and at the same time it was almost representational. The other picture burned with reds. Concentric ellipses filled the background (or foreground, depending upon the interpretation) and enveloped the huddled red figure of a shawled woman.

Jacob's heart leaped when she put her hand upon the bolt of the door. And when Leah entered her smile warmed him as she removed the wrap that had guarded her from the cold.

"Been working hard today?" she asked. He shook his head noncommittally.

"Have you eaten?" He'd been too nervous to eat.

"Well, you must stay healthy in spite of all else," she said. "This evening we'll have the trout."

Jeanne hadn't been in for a couple of days and so Jacob helped Leah cook by filleting the fish. Leah knew of ways to serve the fish stuffed with various interesting things. She added special herbs to bring out the rarest, most succulent tastes.

That night Leah told him that she was pregnant. The news filled him with a sad kind of happiness. He kissed her and told her he'd be to bed soon.

At night after Leah had finished her toilet, she'd placed a shawl over his shoulders as he sat in the progressively colder study. When he heard her climb up the stairs and her bedroom door close and the lock snap, thoughts, visions, dreams and the thousands of faces he'd come to know in the town paraded before him. Wild packs of dogs ran outside through the night.

The life of Jacob's father, like that of many black men, had ended violently. He had been tried and executed for the crime of being born black. The reason for his notoriety in the community (a lot of adults had pointed at him as a child) was baffling and frightening. Thus he grew with the understanding that he was a marked man, but never understanding why. Now he'd been caught stepping outside the laws and customs of his day. He could never lead himself or his family back to safety.

Jacob tried to think when his life had developed the sense of urgency that had put him out of step with the pace of life around him. Most of his acquaintances in the neighborhood and at school believed there was no American or Mississippi crisis. They held the smug belief that mankind is fated to progress, whereas he had come to hold, by his final year of high school, an opposite, radical opinion. He had paced his room nights and came to be seen roaming about the streets constantly in strange company.

The fellows in town he had considered most creative—the ones who could outcurse, outfight, and outdrink anyone in the world and who had plans to become singers, actors, chemists and doctors—grew up to be dope addicts, adulterous fathers of eight children by two women, forlorn faggots and big-time liars, brawlers and drunkards. He'd found Widow Sanders exceedingly brilliant to be able to spend all of her time preaching and healing and cursing people. Gittens, the amiable town drunk, surely had brains. He was able to spend most of his daylight hours sitting on various curbstones lost in thought. The fellows in the town he'd considered most dull were those who stayed in their homes studying all day and who went into the army or to school to prove something or other to their parents.

Jacob thought of himself as having been a child who had lived an ironic life. Every experience contradicted all that had been taught him by teachers, preachers and the adult world. He could see no place for him in life as a Black American. No one had ever told him, "Here, see this land, this house, this industry, this state—when you're grown it will be yours." He had been a child who had suffered from living with the troubles of an adult. Maturing had meant discovering that the oppression he had known as a child would be doubled with age. He had done what he was expected to do. He went to college, picked up a lot of scholarship aid and became a doctor. Until he'd gotten involved in politics, he'd not done anything different than any of the other people in the town he'd known. He'd follow whither life led him just as they did.

What seemed like a hundred years of toughening had brought Jacob to the point, at the age of thirty-five, where he had to rebel from that part of himself which was "white." Perhaps then, he thought, he might become human. Jacob knew that, as in the past, the gut problem was how to deal with his own family and friends. He'd learned that while you might be ducking the bullets of your enemy it need only take a word from a friend to slip the fatal knife into your soul.

When the sun rose its light startled Jacob. He was surprised that the night of wrestling had not exhausted him. He felt free. When Jacob left the house to walk down to the river and watch the steam rise from it as the sun heated its waters he didn't say good-bye to Leah. But he did put a note in the middle of his desk where she'd be sure to find it when she looked for him. In large flowing script, filling the entire piece of stationery, he wrote: "There is no emptiness where you are."

Bang! The sniper's bullet simply and rudely sounded as Jacob stepped onto his porch. He fell back dead, the mark of an assassin on his neck.

Bernard sat in his office at the warehouse talking on the phone to his father at the bank when Art Reid burst in. Bernard knew something singular was wrong, for in Art's eyes he thought he could see fear.

As he hung up Art smiled falsely and said, "Well, I did it."

"Did what?" Bernard asked.

"Took care of that little bit o' business fo' you."

"What you talking about?"

"You know. I killed that nigger Blue."

Bernard's eyes grew big and he leaned forward in his chair and unloosened his tie. "You what?"

"Layed all day and night for the mother in some bushes across the street. When he come out in the mornin' for his paper I dropped him."

"Don't you go around sayin' about I told you to do it. I ain't never told you no such thing."

"But you been talkin' about how we got to do away with the niggers and commies. And, Bernard, you know yourself what Whiteman's been sayin' at meetings lately. I just done what was right."

"You ain't told no one else about killin' for me, have you?" Bernard said, wiping nervous perspiration from his brow—the kind that smells extra sharp.

"You goin' ta take care o' your boy, ain't ya?"

"Of course, of course, but don't tell nobody else nothin'. Nothin' about nothin', do ya hear me?"

Art looked at Bernard with his deceptive little eyes peeking through the bush of his frowning eyebrows.

"Look, Art," Bernard whined. "Why'd you have to do it? We had the niggers in hand. Blue lost the election. Soon I'd of had him eating out of my hand. His practice is ruined. He would've come to us begging soon. You sure he's dead?"

"Have you ever heard of someone I dropped gettin' up and tellin' about it?"

"Who saw you come in here?"

"Nobody, except your secretary and the men out yonder."

"Well, if anybody asks you why you come here today tell 'em that ya come lookin' for a job in the warehouse."

"You gonna take care o' me Bernie?"

"I had nothing to do with your crime and I don't want to get mixed up in it."

"You are a white man, ain't ya Bernie?"

Bernard stood and went into his pocket. While looking Art in the face, without speaking, Bernard took out his wallet and peeled off a couple of hundred. "You better take a vacation, Art. New York, or Mexico. When you get there let me know where you are and I'll send more."

Taking the money and grabbing Bernard's hand, Art said, "I knew you'd come through, Bernie."

As Art moved from the room, the awesome presence like that about a killer whale's feeding ground left with him. Bernard sat down, punching one hand into another. He hadn't planned to kill Jacob in that particular manner. Now he'd have to give serious thought to having someone kill Art or Art would implicate him in the crime. He talked too much.

The tight-assed secretary bounced into the office, disturbingly close to Bernard. He would have to take care of that problem immediately. He locked the door to the room and sat on the couch. She smiled and dropped down beside him.